ACCLAIM FOR JEFF SMITH'S

Named an all-time top ten graphic novel by **Time** *magazine.*

"As sweeping as the 'Lord of the Rings' cycle, but much funnier." —*Andrew Arnold,* **Time.com**

★*"This is first-class kid lit: exciting, funny, scary, and resonant enough that it will stick with readers for a long time."* —**Publishers Weekly,** *starred review*

"One of the best kids' comics ever." —**Vibe** *magazine*

*"***BONE** *is storytelling at its best, full of endearing, flawed characters whose adventures run the gamut from hilarious whimsy . . . to thrilling drama."* —**Entertainment Weekly**

"[This] sprawling, mythic comic is spectacular." —**SPIN** *magazine*

"Jeff Smith's cartoons are irresistible. Every gorgeous sweep of his brush speaks volumes." —*Frank Miller, creator of* **Sin City**

OTHER *BONE* BOOKS

Out from Boneville

The Great Cow Race

Eyes of the Storm

The Dragonslayer

Rock Jaw: Master of the Eastern Border

Old Man's Cave

GHOST CIRCLES

BY JEFF SMITH

WITH COLOR BY STEVE HAMAKER

An Imprint of

SCHOLASTIC

New York   Toronto   London   Auckland   Sydney   Mexico City   New Delhi   Hong Kong   Buenos Aires

All rights reserved. Published by Graphix, an imprint of Scholastic Inc., *Publishers since 1920.* SCHOLASTIC, GRAPHIX, and associated logos are trademarks and/or registered trademarks of Scholastic Inc.

Library of Congress Catalog Card Number 9568403.
ISBN-13 978-0-439-70629-2 — ISBN-10 0-439-70629-7 (hardcover)
ISBN 0-439-70634-3 (paperback)

ACKNOWLEDGMENTS
Harvestar Family Crest designed by Charles Vess
Map of *The Valley* by Mark Crilley
Color by Steve Hamaker

10 9 8 7 6 5 4 3 2 1   08 09 10
First Scholastic edition, February 2008
Book design by David Saylor
Printed in Singapore 46

This book is for Charles Vess

CONTENTS

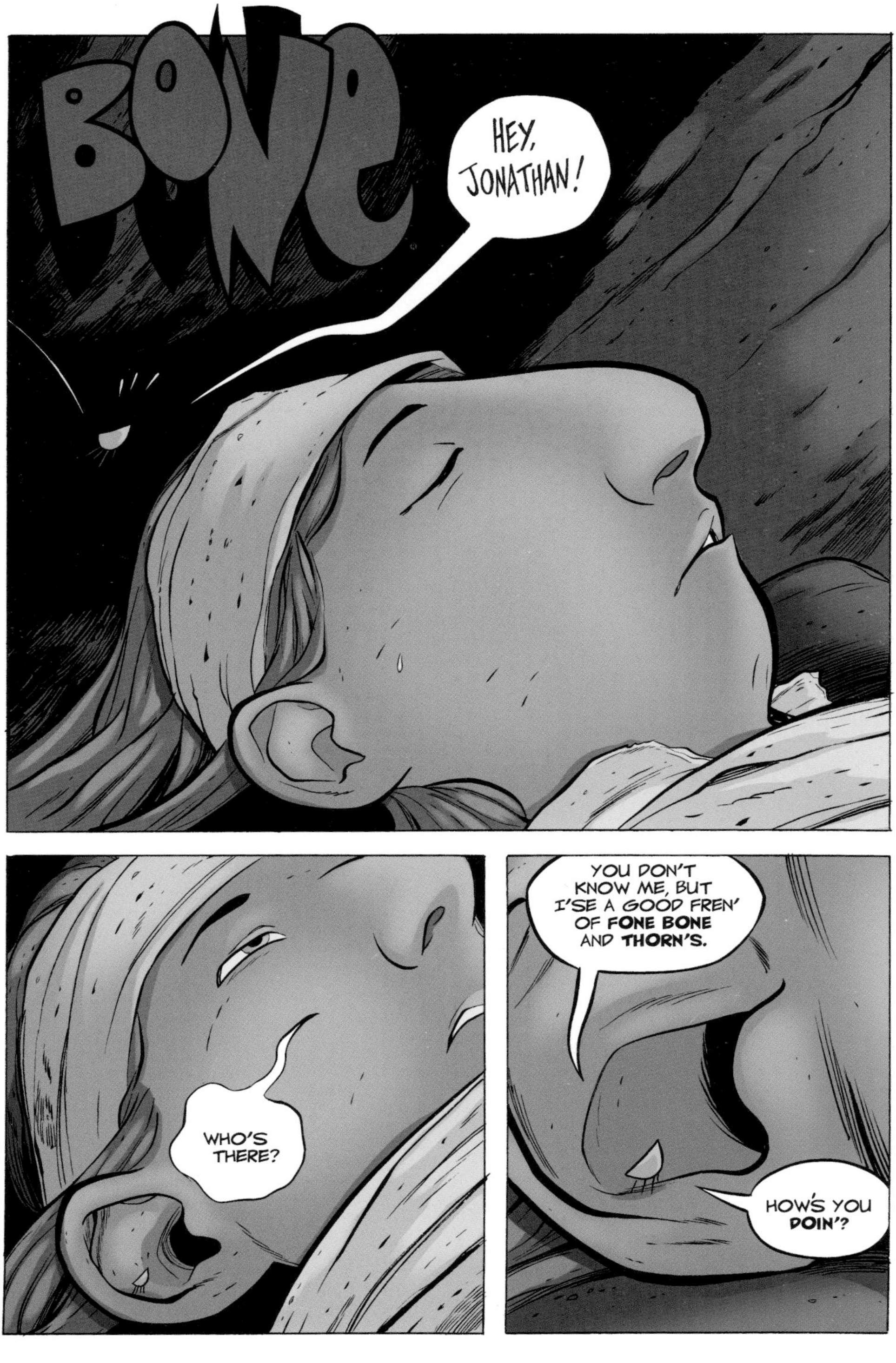
BONE
HEY, JONATHAN!
WHO'S THERE?
YOU DON'T KNOW ME, BUT I'SE A GOOD FREN' OF **FONE BONE** AND **THORN'S.**
HOW'S YOU **DOIN'**?

NOT TOO GOOD.

I'SE **REAL** SORRY TO HEAR THAT. THORN WILL BE, TOO.

LISTEN, JON - - THORN SENT ME AHEAD TO FIND GRAN'MA BEN AN' THE DRAGONS - - TO TELL 'EM THAT THORN'S COMIN' TO **JOIN** 'EM.

BUT JON - - I CAN'T FIND NO **DRAGONS** - - I CAN'T FIND NO GRAN'MA BENS! AN' I THOUGHT **THORNY'D** BE HERE BY **NOW**.

WHERE **IS** EVERYBODY?

THE DRAGONS . . . HAVE GONE UNDERGROUND FOR GOOD. GRAN'MA SAID SO.

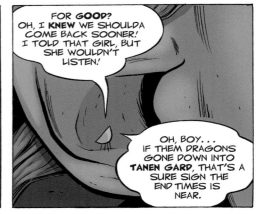

FOR **GOOD?** OH, I **KNEW** WE SHOULDA COME BACK SOONER! I TOLD THAT GIRL, BUT SHE WOULDN'T LISTEN!

OH, BOY. . . IF THEM DRAGONS GONE DOWN INTO **TANEN GARD**, THAT'S A SURE SIGN THE END TIMES IS NEAR.

I GOT TO FIND GRAN'MA BEN! OR **LUCIUS!** YOU KNOW WHERE LUCIUS IS, JONNY?

THEY DISAPPEARED. EVERYBODY SAYS LUCIUS DONE IT.

DONE WHAT?

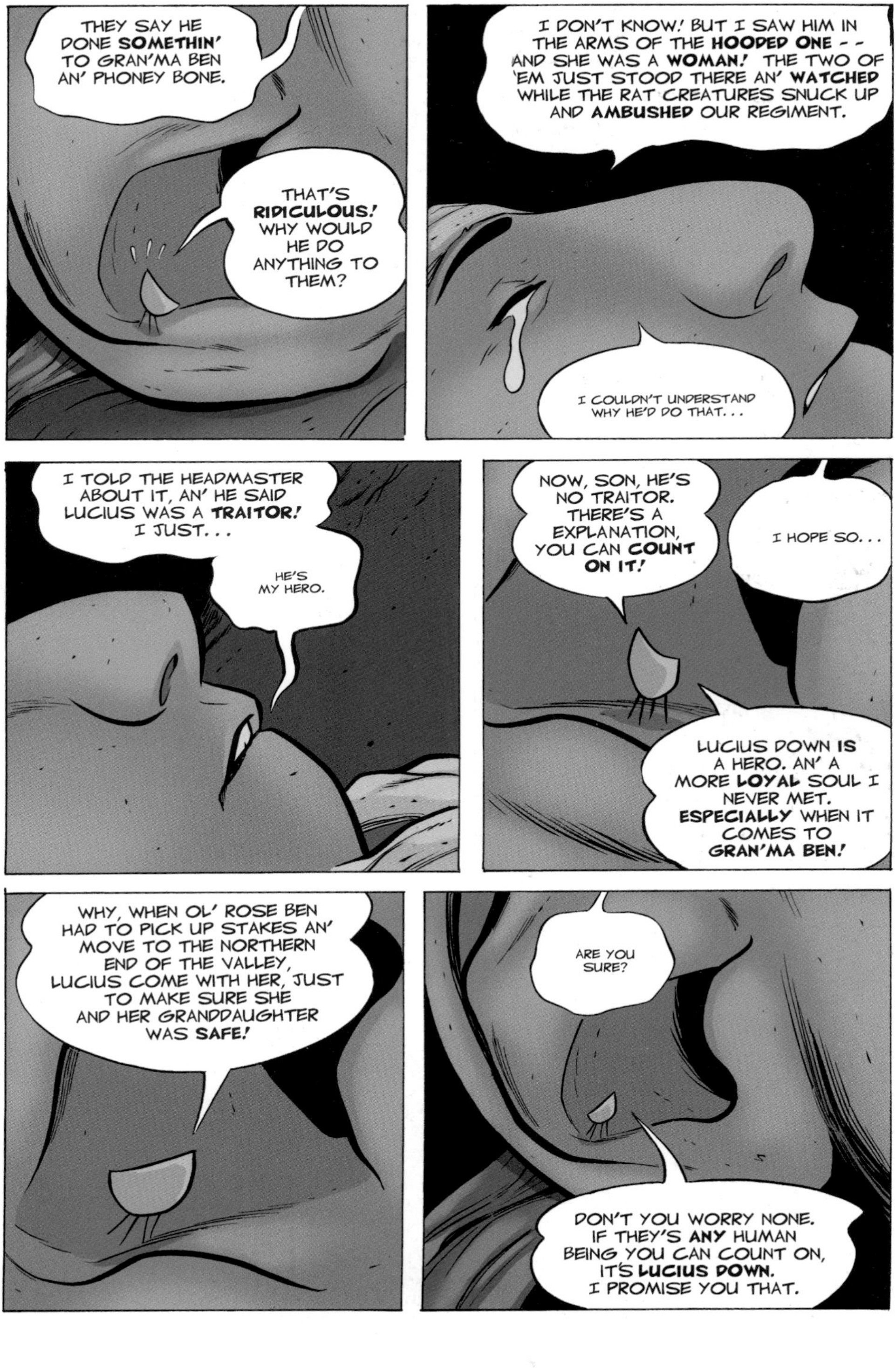
THEY SAY HE DONE SOMETHIN' TO GRAN'MA BEN AN' PHONEY BONE.
THAT'S RIDICULOUS! WHY WOULD HE DO ANYTHING TO THEM?
I DON'T KNOW! BUT I SAW HIM IN THE ARMS OF THE HOODED ONE - - AND SHE WAS A WOMAN! THE TWO OF 'EM JUST STOOD THERE AN' WATCHED WHILE THE RAT CREATURES SNUCK UP AND AMBUSHED OUR REGIMENT.
I COULDN'T UNDERSTAND WHY HE'D DO THAT. . .
I TOLD THE HEADMASTER ABOUT IT, AN' HE SAID LUCIUS WAS A TRAITOR! I JUST. . .
HE'S MY HERO.
NOW, SON, HE'S NO TRAITOR. THERE'S A EXPLANATION, YOU CAN COUNT ON IT!
I HOPE SO. . .
LUCIUS DOWN IS A HERO. AN' A MORE LOYAL SOUL I NEVER MET. ESPECIALLY WHEN IT COMES TO GRAN'MA BEN!
WHY, WHEN OL' ROSE BEN HAD TO PICK UP STAKES AN' MOVE TO THE NORTHERN END OF THE VALLEY, LUCIUS COME WITH HER, JUST TO MAKE SURE SHE AND HER GRANDDAUGHTER WAS SAFE!
ARE YOU SURE?
DON'T YOU WORRY NONE. IF THEY'S ANY HUMAN BEING YOU CAN COUNT ON, IT'S LUCIUS DOWN. I PROMISE YOU THAT.

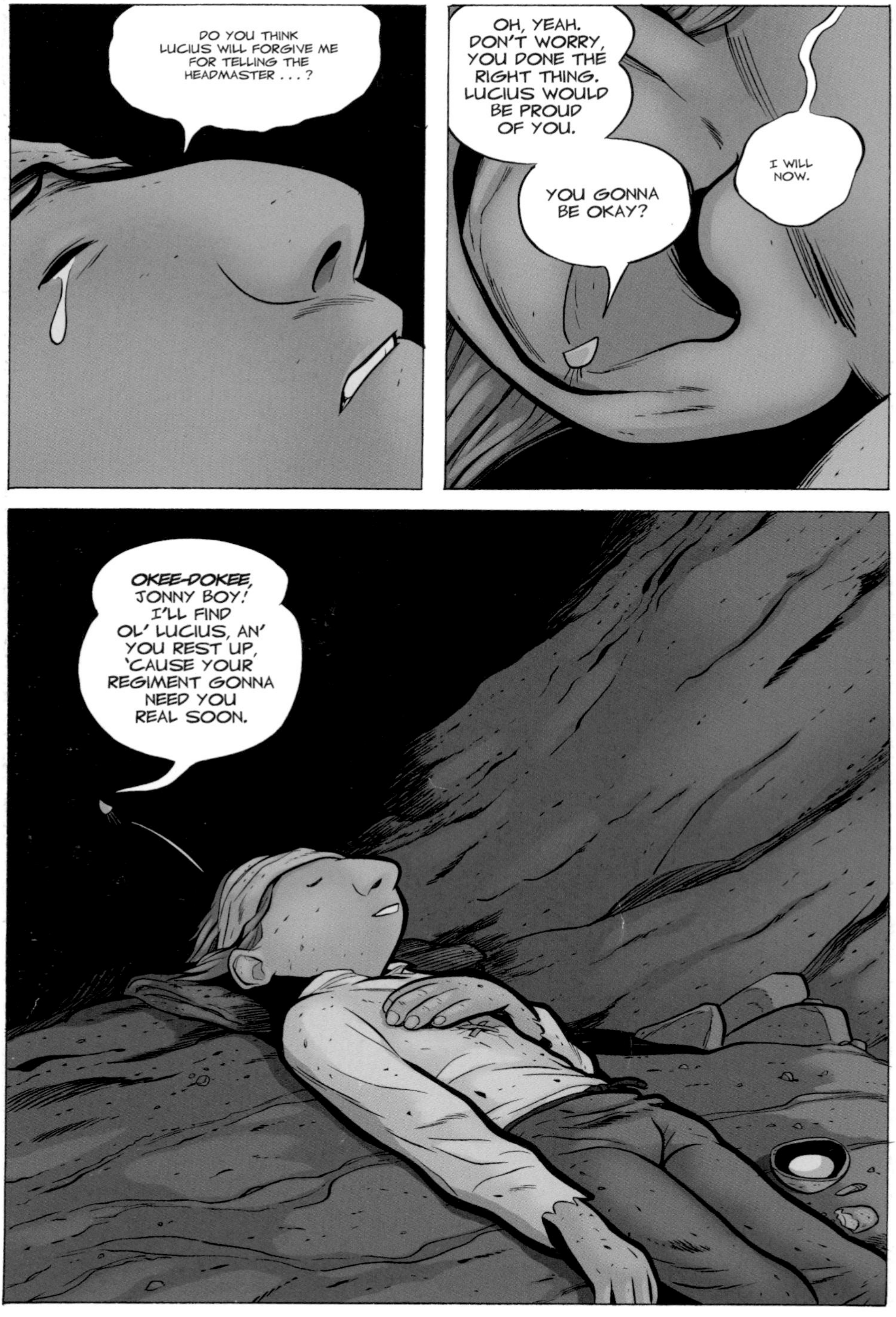
DO YOU THINK LUCIUS WILL FORGIVE ME FOR TELLING THE HEADMASTER . . . ?
OH, YEAH. DON'T WORRY, YOU DONE THE RIGHT THING. LUCIUS WOULD BE PROUD OF YOU.
YOU GONNA BE OKAY?
I WILL NOW.
OKEE-DOKEE, JONNY BOY! I'LL FIND OL' LUCIUS, AN' YOU REST UP, 'CAUSE YOUR REGIMENT GONNA NEED YOU REAL SOON.

GHOST CIRCLES

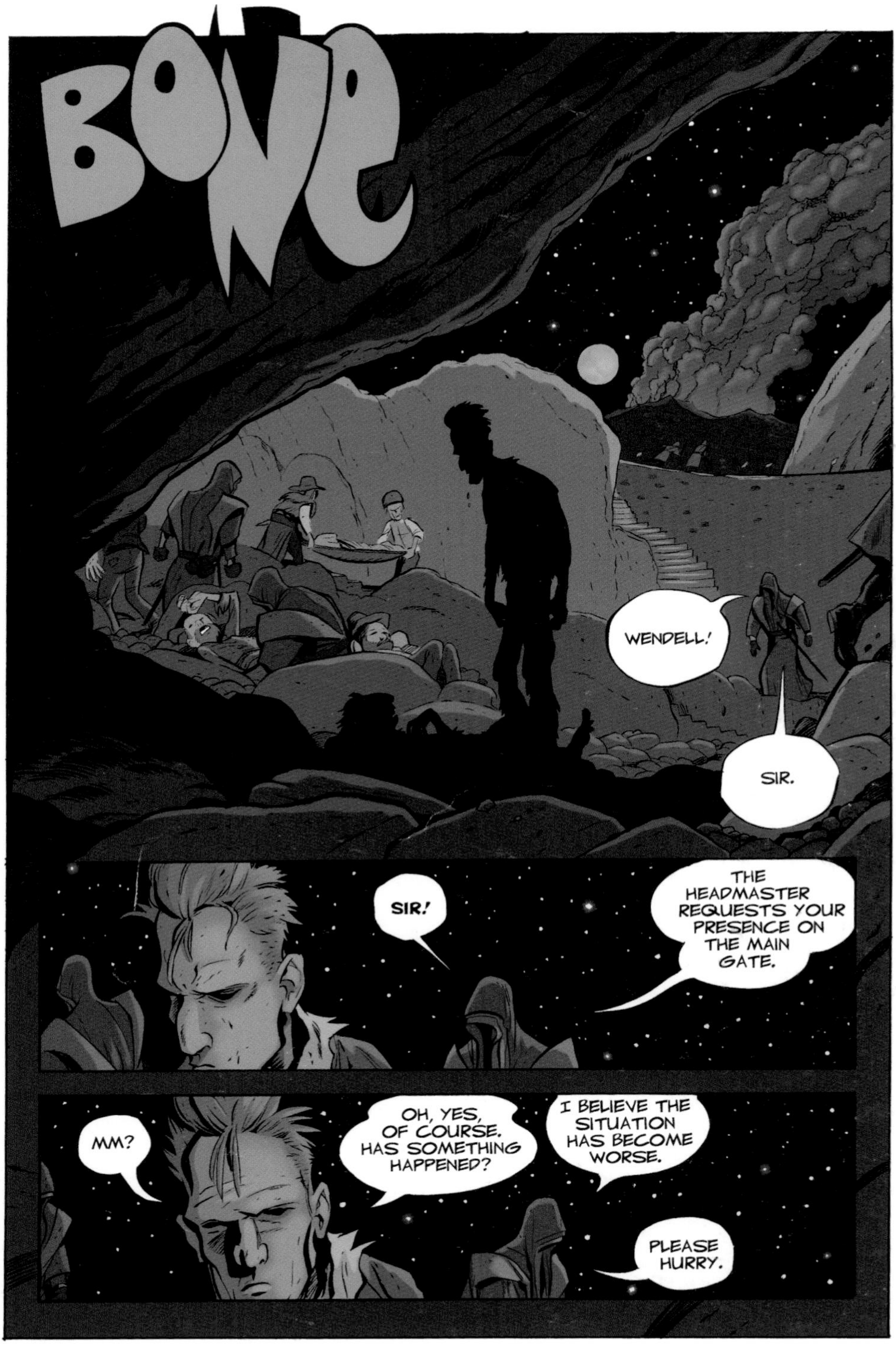
BONE
WENDELL!
SIR.
SIR!
THE HEADMASTER REQUESTS YOUR PRESENCE ON THE MAIN GATE.
MM?
OH, YES, OF COURSE. HAS SOMETHING HAPPENED?
I BELIEVE THE SITUATION HAS BECOME WORSE.
PLEASE HURRY.

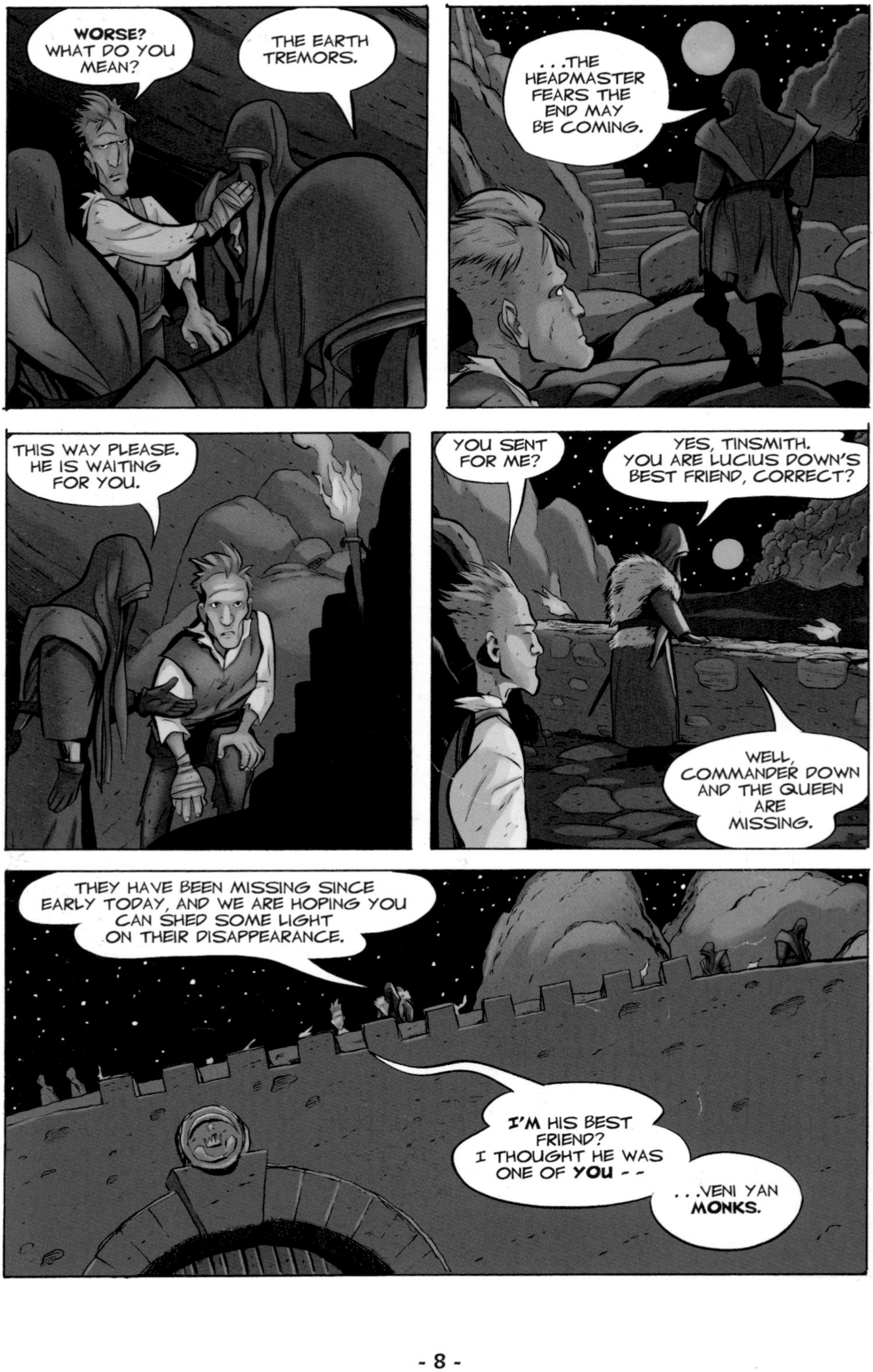
WORSE? WHAT DO YOU MEAN?
THE EARTH TREMORS.
. . .THE HEADMASTER FEARS THE END MAY BE COMING.
THIS WAY PLEASE. HE IS WAITING FOR YOU.
YOU SENT FOR ME?
YES, TINSMITH. YOU ARE LUCIUS DOWN'S BEST FRIEND, CORRECT?
WELL, COMMANDER DOWN AND THE QUEEN ARE MISSING.
THEY HAVE BEEN MISSING SINCE EARLY TODAY, AND WE ARE HOPING YOU CAN SHED SOME LIGHT ON THEIR DISAPPEARANCE.
I'M HIS BEST FRIEND? I THOUGHT HE WAS ONE OF YOU - -
. . .VENI YAN MONKS.

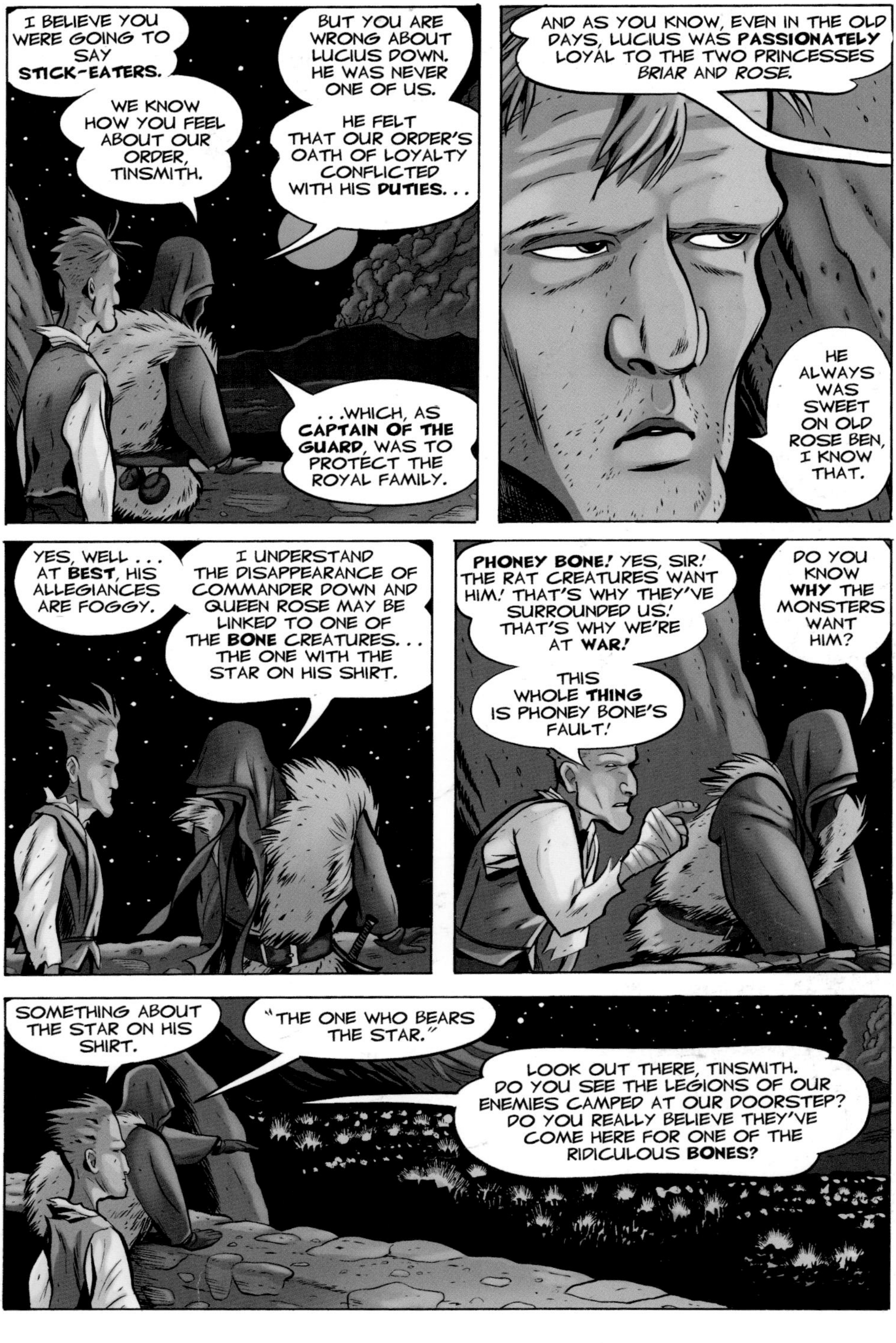
I BELIEVE YOU WERE GOING TO SAY **STICK-EATERS.**
WE KNOW HOW YOU FEEL ABOUT OUR ORDER, TINSMITH.
BUT YOU ARE WRONG ABOUT LUCIUS DOWN. HE WAS NEVER ONE OF US.
HE FELT THAT OUR ORDER'S OATH OF LOYALTY CONFLICTED WITH HIS **DUTIES**. . .
. . .WHICH, AS **CAPTAIN OF THE GUARD**, WAS TO PROTECT THE ROYAL FAMILY.
AND AS YOU KNOW, EVEN IN THE OLD DAYS, LUCIUS WAS **PASSIONATELY** LOYAL TO THE TWO PRINCESSES *BRIAR* AND *ROSE*.
HE ALWAYS WAS SWEET ON OLD ROSE BEN, I KNOW THAT.
YES, WELL . . . AT **BEST**, HIS ALLEGIANCES ARE FOGGY.
I UNDERSTAND THE DISAPPEARANCE OF COMMANDER DOWN AND QUEEN ROSE MAY BE LINKED TO ONE OF THE **BONE** CREATURES. . . THE ONE WITH THE STAR ON HIS SHIRT.
PHONEY BONE! YES, SIR! THE RAT CREATURES WANT HIM! THAT'S WHY THEY'VE SURROUNDED US! THAT'S WHY WE'RE AT **WAR!**
THIS WHOLE **THING** IS PHONEY BONE'S FAULT!
DO YOU KNOW **WHY** THE MONSTERS WANT HIM?
SOMETHING ABOUT THE STAR ON HIS SHIRT.
"THE ONE WHO BEARS THE STAR."
LOOK OUT THERE, TINSMITH. DO YOU SEE THE LEGIONS OF OUR ENEMIES CAMPED AT OUR DOORSTEP? DO YOU REALLY BELIEVE THEY'VE COME HERE FOR ONE OF THE RIDICULOUS **BONES?**

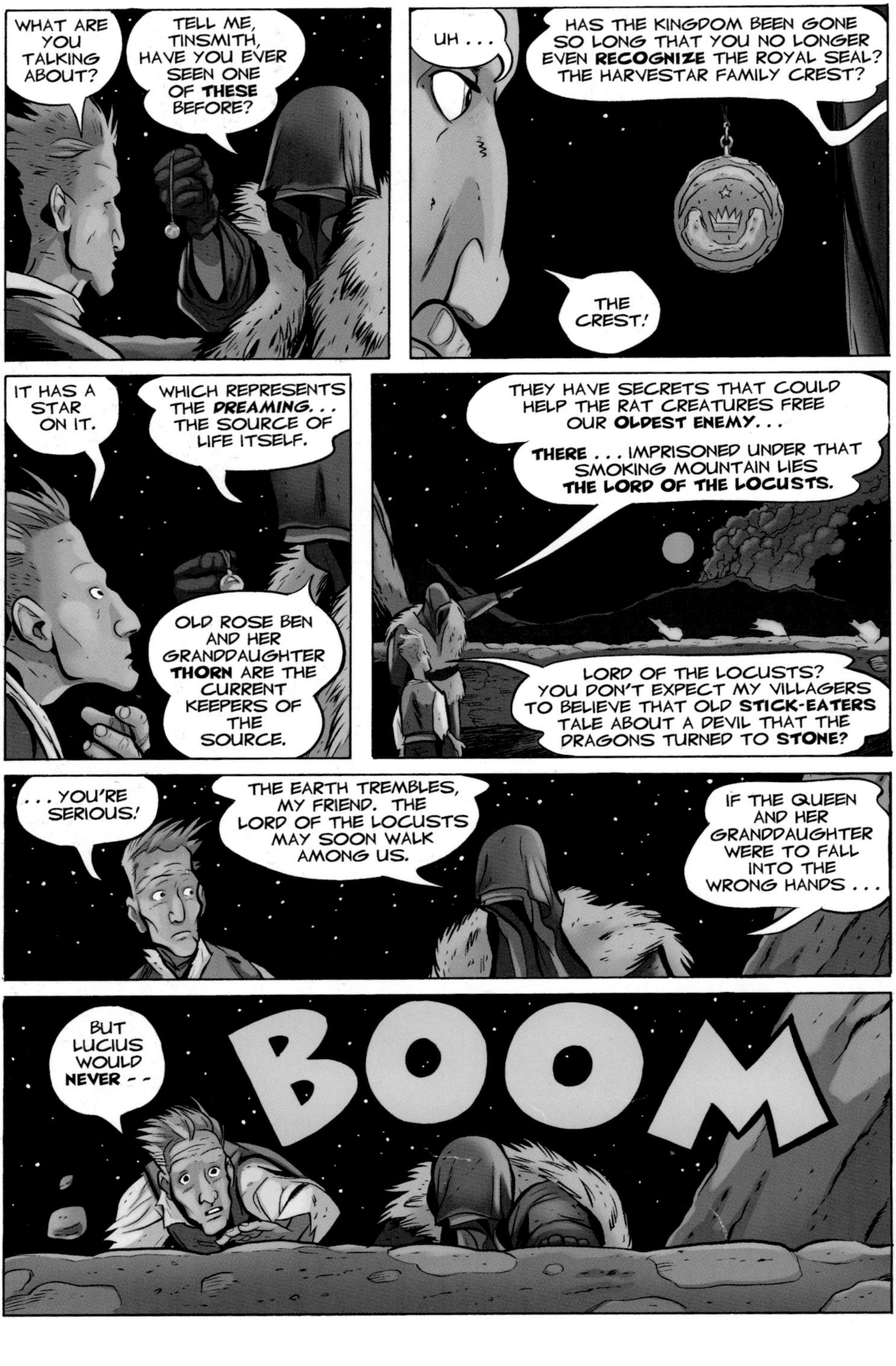
WHAT ARE YOU TALKING ABOUT?
TELL ME, TINSMITH, HAVE YOU EVER SEEN ONE OF **THESE** BEFORE?
UH . . .
HAS THE KINGDOM BEEN GONE SO LONG THAT YOU NO LONGER EVEN **RECOGNIZE** THE ROYAL SEAL? THE HARVESTAR FAMILY CREST?
THE CREST!
IT HAS A STAR ON IT.
WHICH REPRESENTS THE ***DREAMING*. . .** THE SOURCE OF LIFE ITSELF.
OLD ROSE BEN AND HER GRANDDAUGHTER **THORN** ARE THE CURRENT KEEPERS OF THE SOURCE.
THEY HAVE SECRETS THAT COULD HELP THE RAT CREATURES FREE OUR **OLDEST ENEMY** . . .
THERE . . . IMPRISONED UNDER THAT SMOKING MOUNTAIN LIES **THE LORD OF THE LOCUSTS.**
LORD OF THE LOCUSTS? YOU DON'T EXPECT MY VILLAGERS TO BELIEVE THAT OLD **STICK-EATERS** TALE ABOUT A DEVIL THAT THE DRAGONS TURNED TO **STONE?**
. . . YOU'RE SERIOUS!
THE EARTH TREMBLES, MY FRIEND. THE LORD OF THE LOCUSTS MAY SOON WALK AMONG US.
IF THE QUEEN AND HER GRANDDAUGHTER WERE TO FALL INTO THE WRONG HANDS . . .
BUT LUCIUS WOULD **NEVER** - -
BOOM

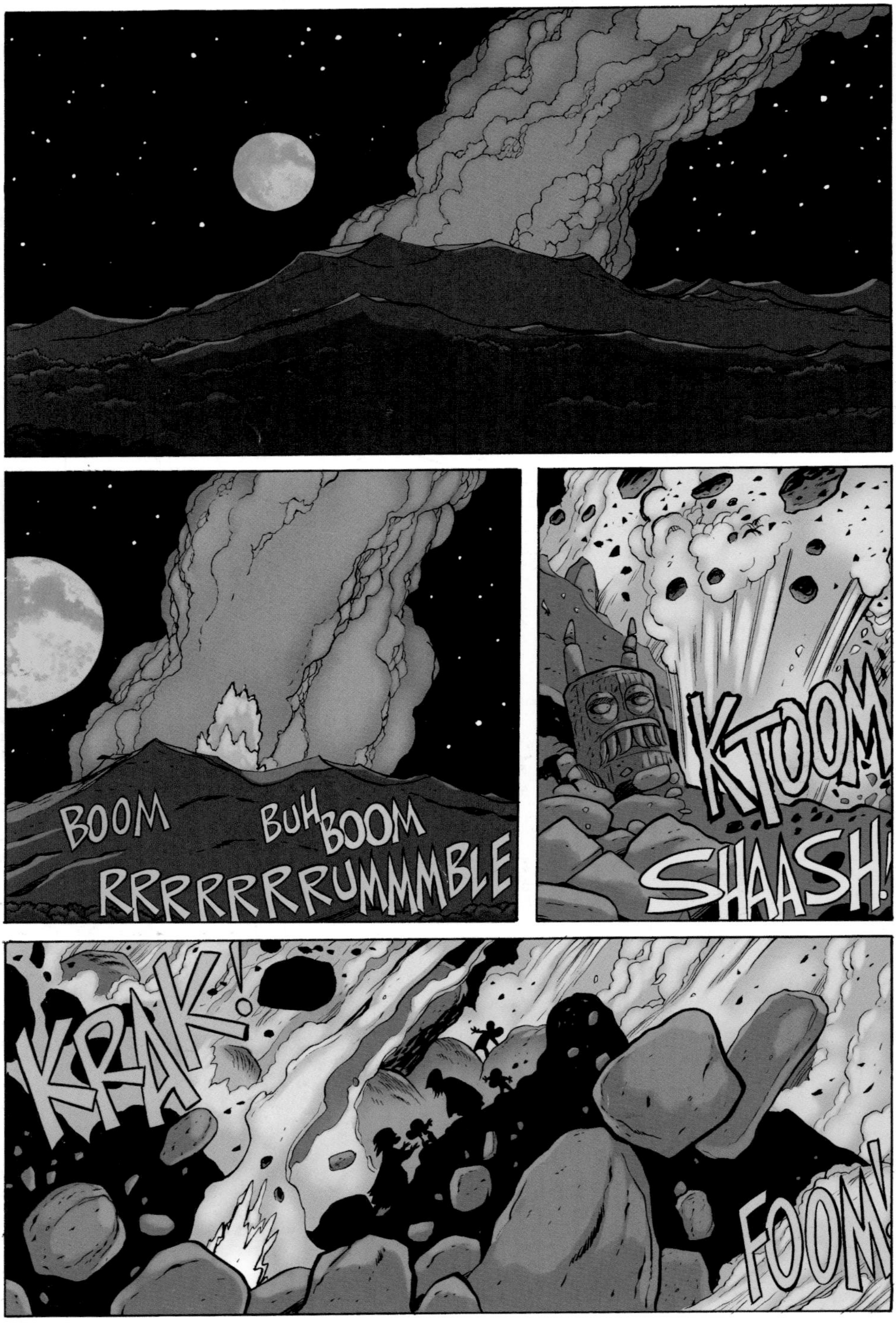
BOOM
BUH BOOM
RRRRRRRUMMMBLE
KTOOM
SHAASH!
KRAK!
FOOM!

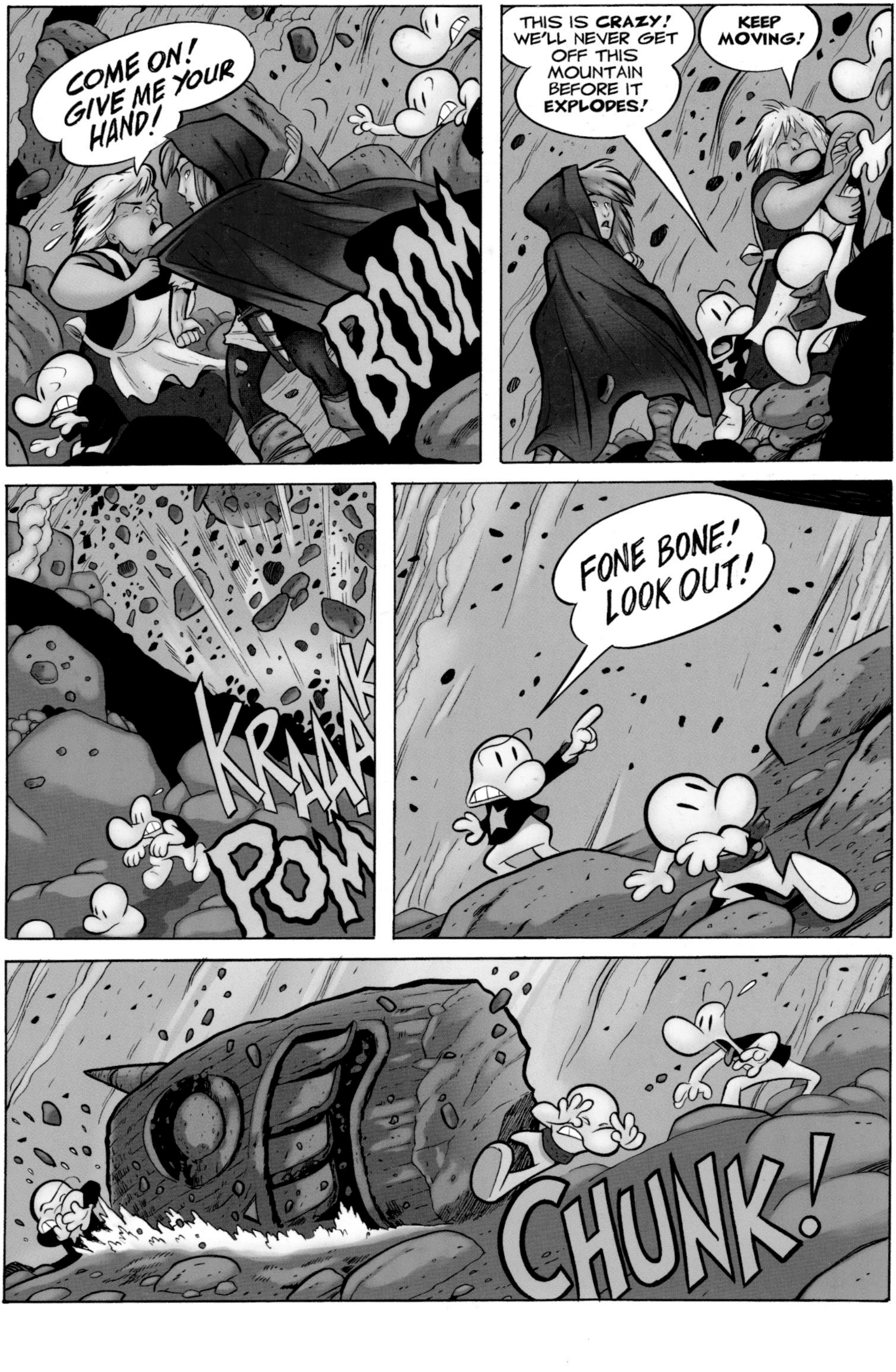
COME ON! GIVE ME YOUR HAND!
BOOM
THIS IS CRAZY! WE'LL NEVER GET OFF THIS MOUNTAIN BEFORE IT EXPLODES!
KEEP MOVING!
KRAAAK
POM
FONE BONE! LOOK OUT!
CHUNK!

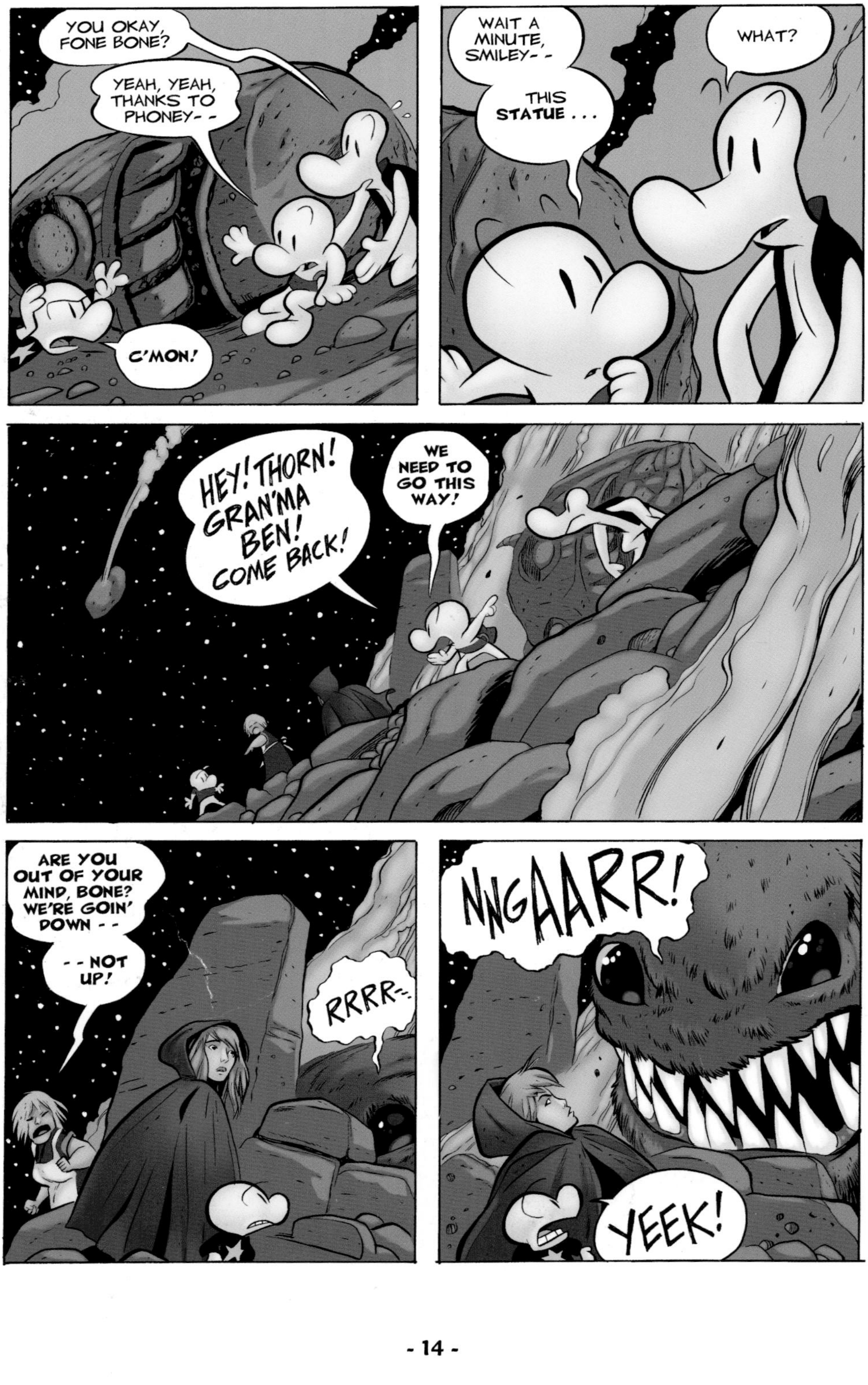
YOU OKAY, FONE BONE?
YEAH, YEAH, THANKS TO PHONEY- -
C'MON!
WAIT A MINUTE, SMILEY- -
THIS STATUE . . .
WHAT?
HEY! THORN! GRAN'MA BEN! COME BACK!
WE NEED TO GO THIS WAY!
ARE YOU OUT OF YOUR MIND, BONE? WE'RE GOIN' DOWN - -
- - NOT UP!
RRRR
NNGAARR!
YEEK!

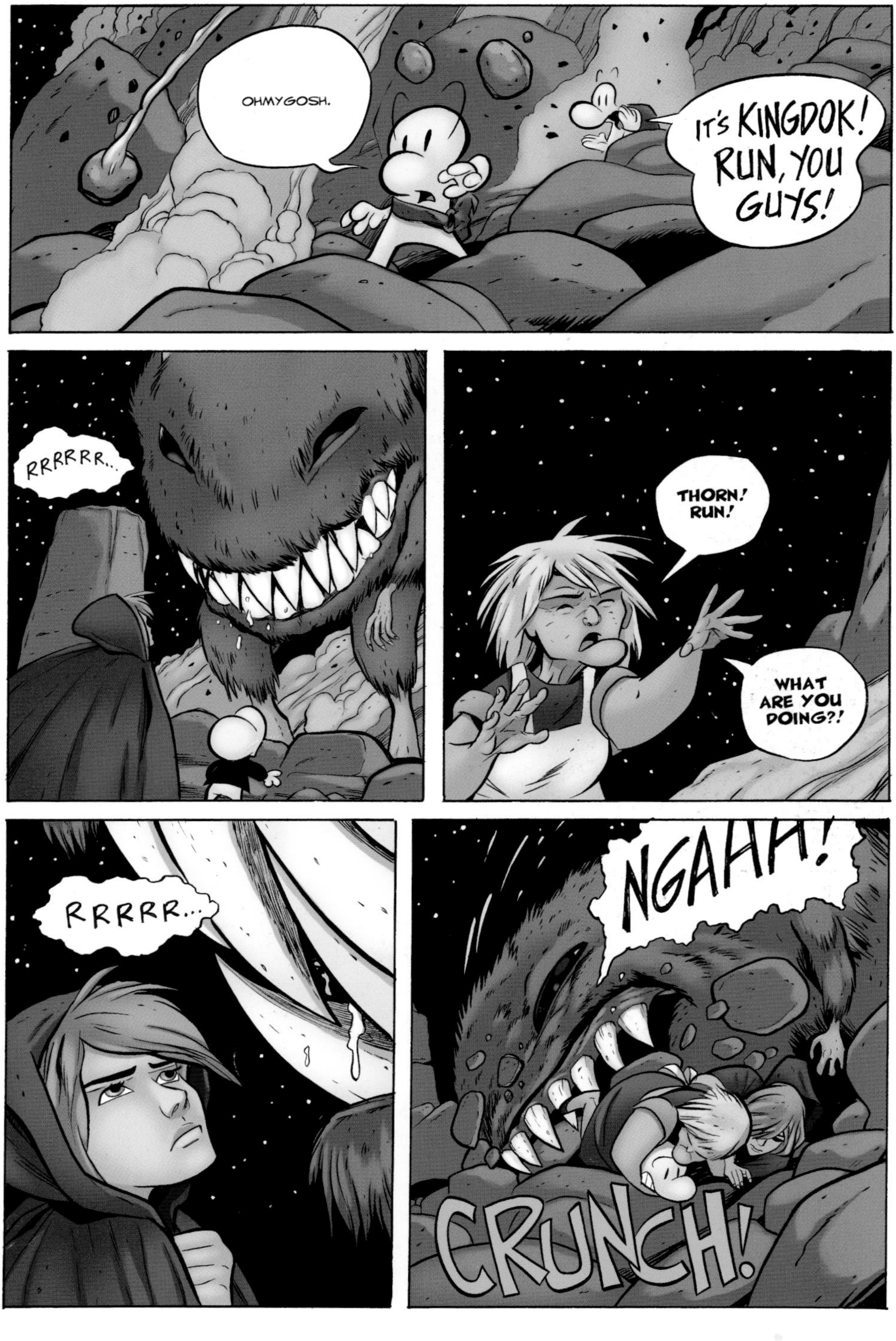
OHMYGOSH.
IT'S KINGDOK! RUN, YOU GUYS!
RRRRRR...
THORN! RUN!
WHAT ARE YOU DOING?!
RRRRR...
NGAHH!
CRUNCH!

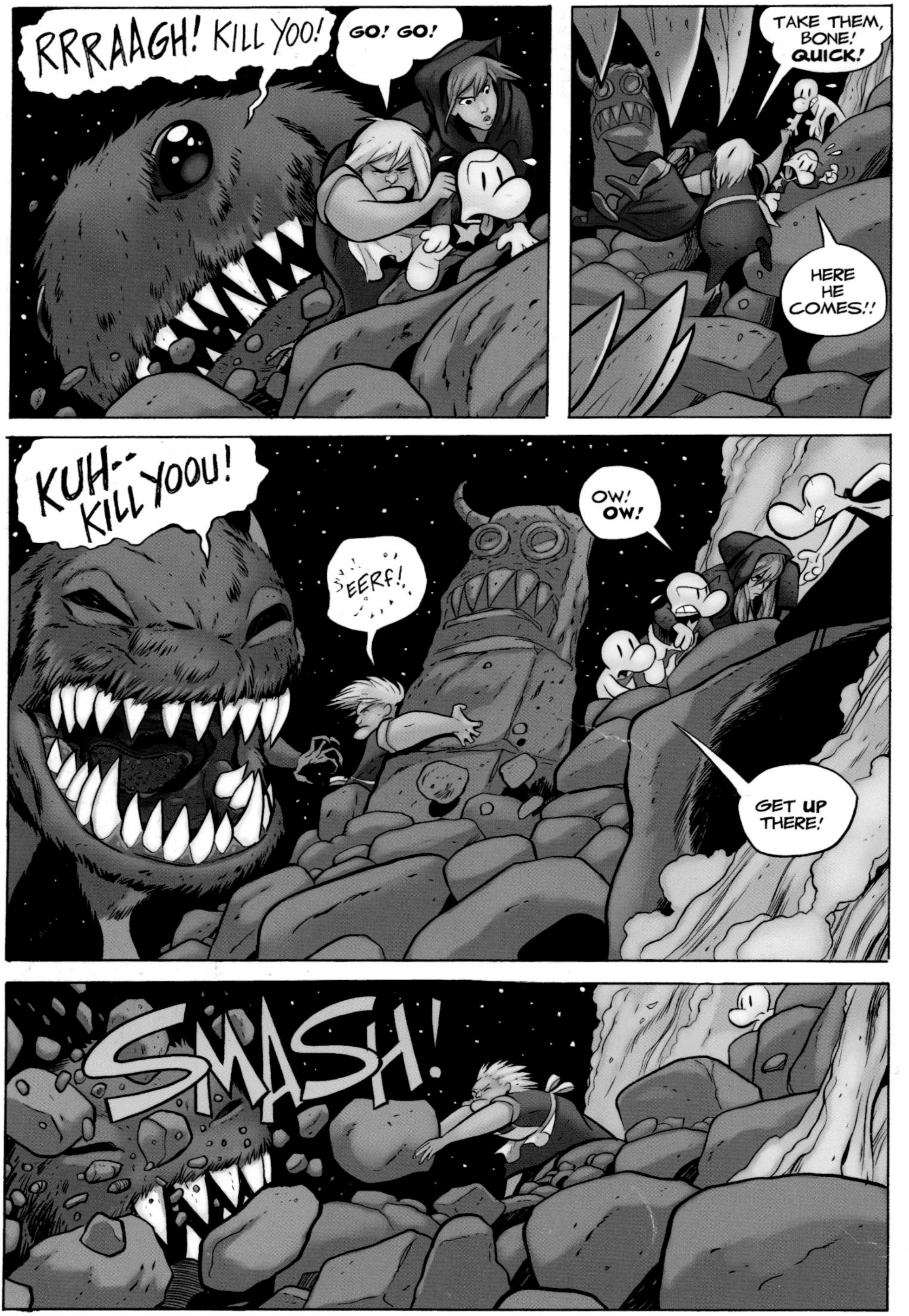
RRRAAGH! KILL YOO!
GO! GO!
TAKE THEM, BONE! QUICK!
HERE HE COMES!!
KUH-- KILL YOOU!
EERF!
OW! OW!
GET UP THERE!
SMASH!

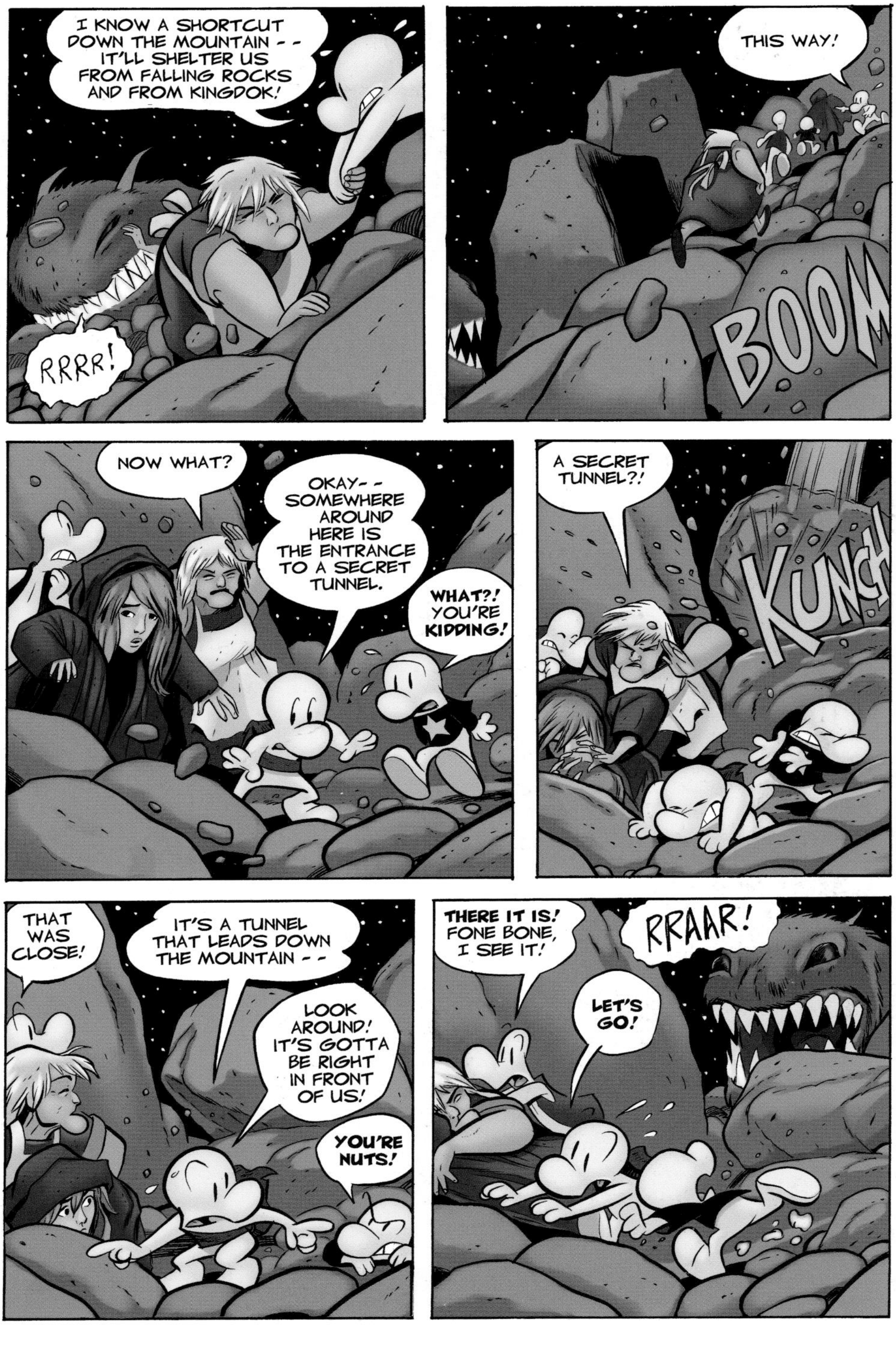
I KNOW A SHORTCUT DOWN THE MOUNTAIN - - IT'LL SHELTER US FROM FALLING ROCKS AND FROM KINGDOK!
RRRR!
THIS WAY!
BOOM
NOW WHAT?
OKAY- - SOMEWHERE AROUND HERE IS THE ENTRANCE TO A SECRET TUNNEL.
WHAT?! YOU'RE KIDDING!
A SECRET TUNNEL?!
KUNCH
THAT WAS CLOSE!
IT'S A TUNNEL THAT LEADS DOWN THE MOUNTAIN - -
LOOK AROUND! IT'S GOTTA BE RIGHT IN FRONT OF US!
YOU'RE NUTS!
THERE IT IS! FONE BONE, I SEE IT!
RRAAR!
LET'S GO!

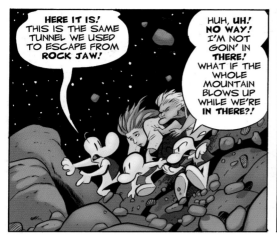

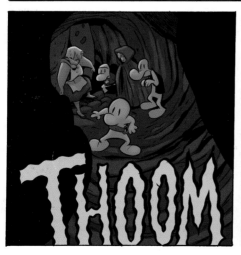

WELL... UH... I GUESS WE HAVE TO GO DOWN THEN.

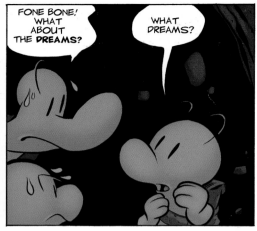

FONE BONE! WHAT ABOUT THE **DREAMS**?

WHAT DREAMS?

DON'T YOU **REMEMBER**? THIS TUNNEL LEADS TO THE OLD **RAT CREATURE TEMPLE**!

OH, MY GOSH! THAT'S RIGHT! AND WE ALL BEGAN TO **HALLUCINATE**!

OH, GREAT.

GRAN'MA! SMILEY AND I HAVE BEEN HERE BEFORE. THERE'S A GOOD CHANCE THAT IF WE GO INTO THIS TUNNEL, WE --

WE'LL BE OVERWHELMED BY **NIGHTMARES**, I KNOW...

I'VE BEEN HERE BEFORE AS WELL. A LONG, LONG TIME AGO.

THOOM

THERE'S THAT NOISE AGAIN!

WHAT THE HECK **IS** THAT?

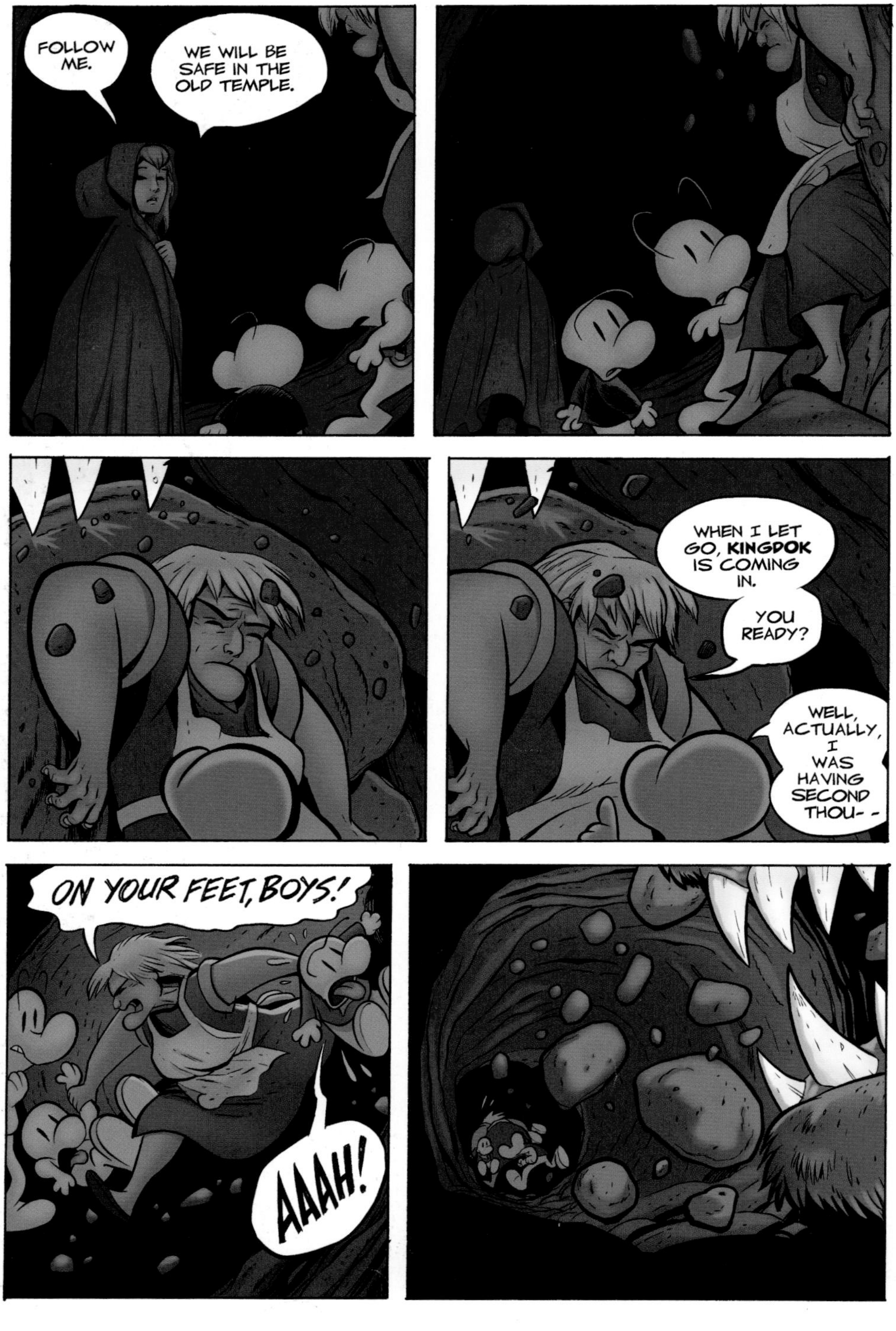
FOLLOW ME.
WE WILL BE SAFE IN THE OLD TEMPLE.
WHEN I LET GO, KINGDOK IS COMING IN.
YOU READY?
WELL, ACTUALLY, I WAS HAVING SECOND THOU- -
ON YOUR FEET, BOYS!
AAAH!

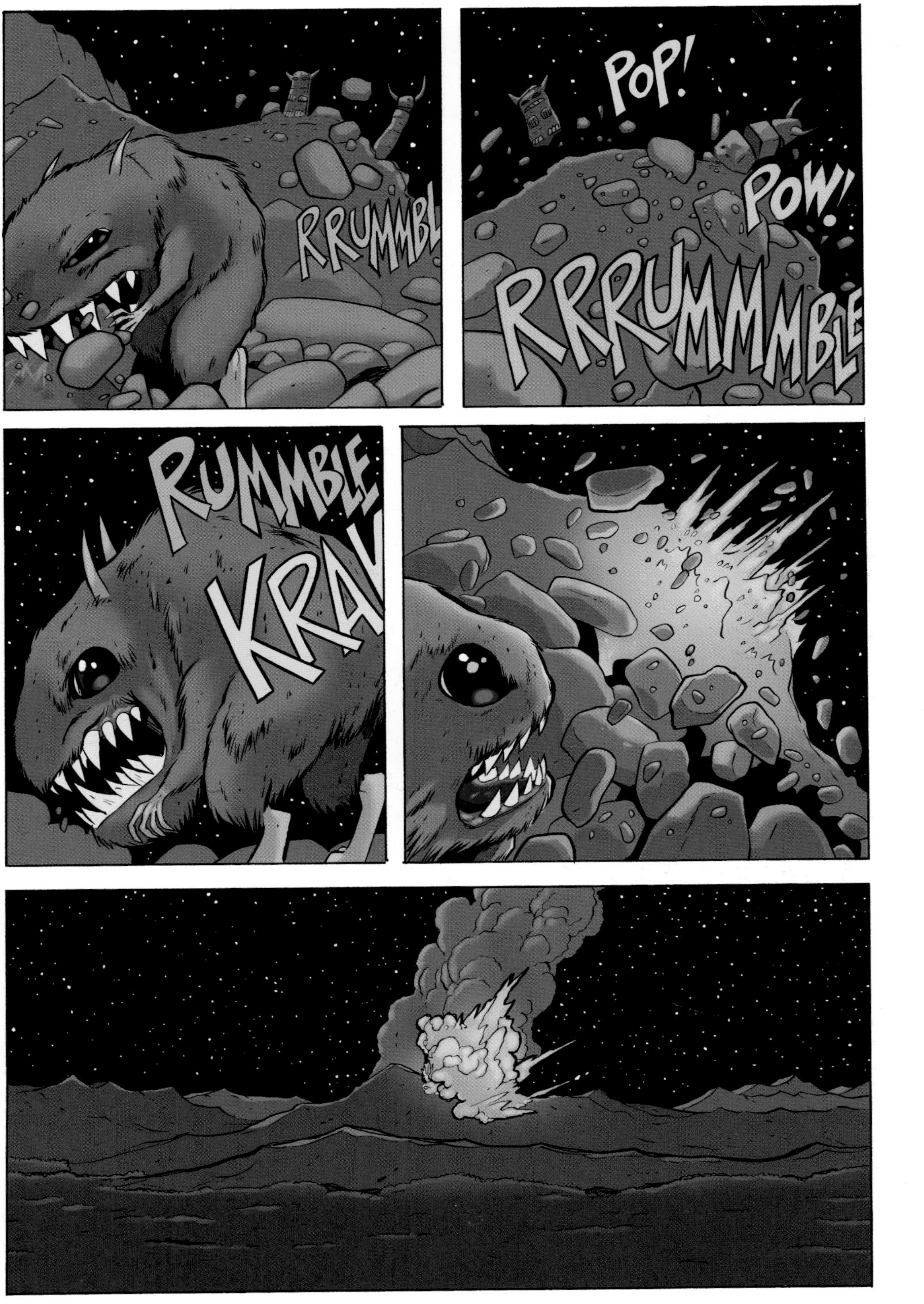
RRUMMBL
POP!
POW!
RRRUMMMMBLE
RUMMBLE
KRA

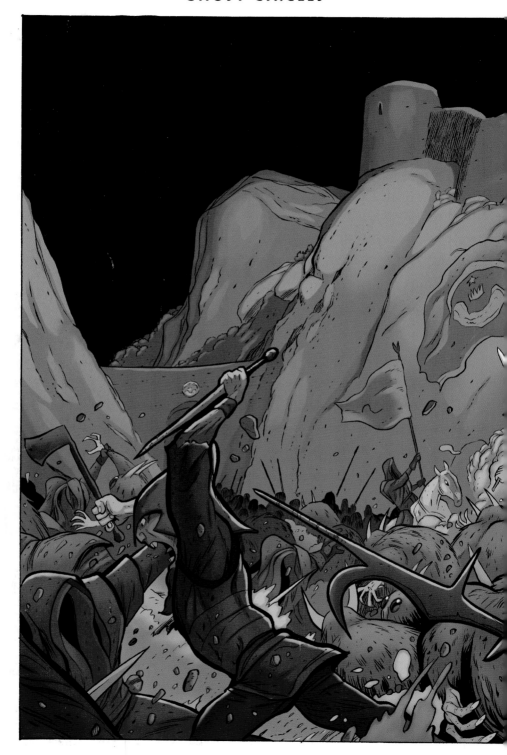

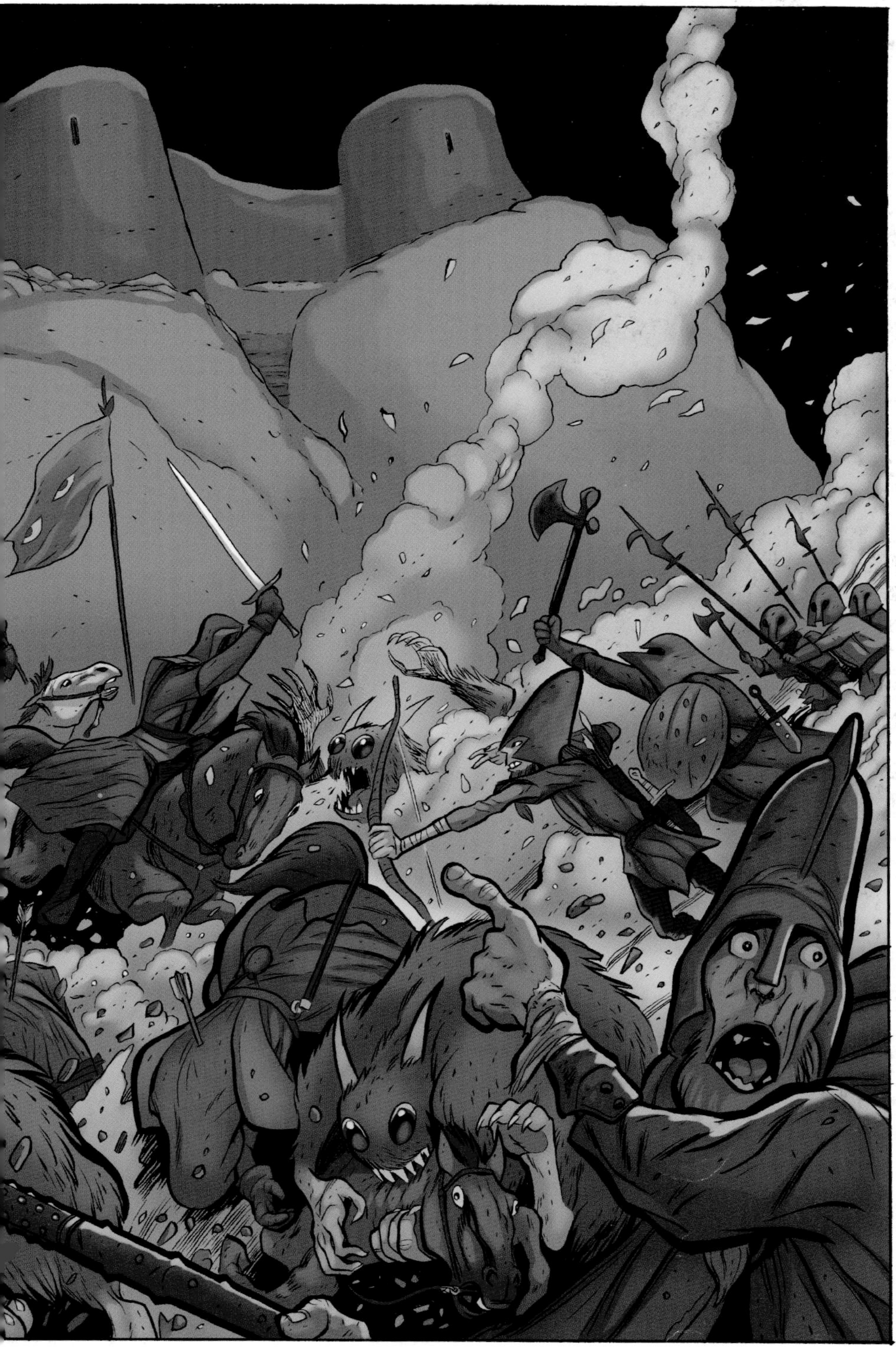

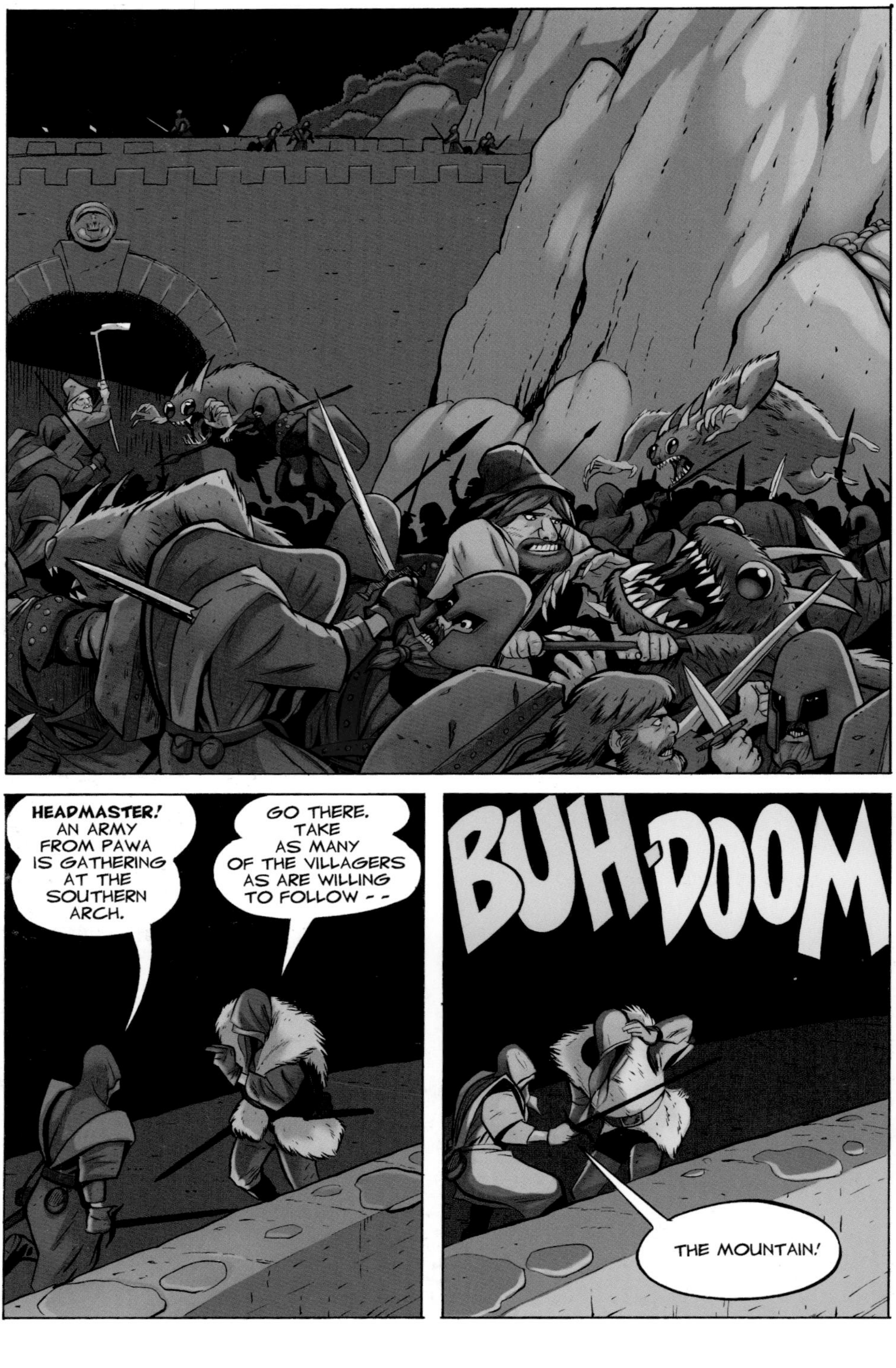
HEADMASTER! AN ARMY FROM PAWA IS GATHERING AT THE SOUTHERN ARCH.
GO THERE. TAKE AS MANY OF THE VILLAGERS AS ARE WILLING TO FOLLOW - -
BUH-DOOM
THE MOUNTAIN!

LOOK AT THAT.

HEADMASTER - -

THE TIME IS COME.

"GREAT DARKNESS FALLS ACROSS OUR GENERATION. MAY WE BE EQUAL TO THE BURDEN."

WHAT ARE YOUR ORDERS?

THE ANCIENT LORD WILL MOVE SWIFTLY ACROSS THE VALLEY . . .

GATHER ALL THE VILLAGERS INTO THE CAVE. THEN PULL OUR MEN BACK. WE DON'T HAVE MUCH TIME TO REACH SHELTER.

WHAT ABOUT THE ATTACK ON THE SOUTHERN ARCH?

IT NO LONGER MATTERS.

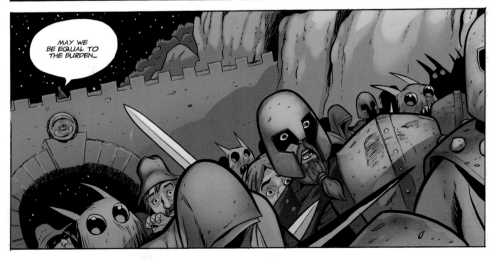

MAY WE BE EQUAL TO THE BURDEN...

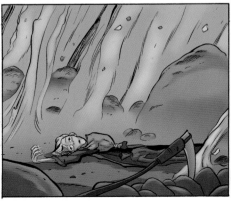

. . . *BRIAR* . . .

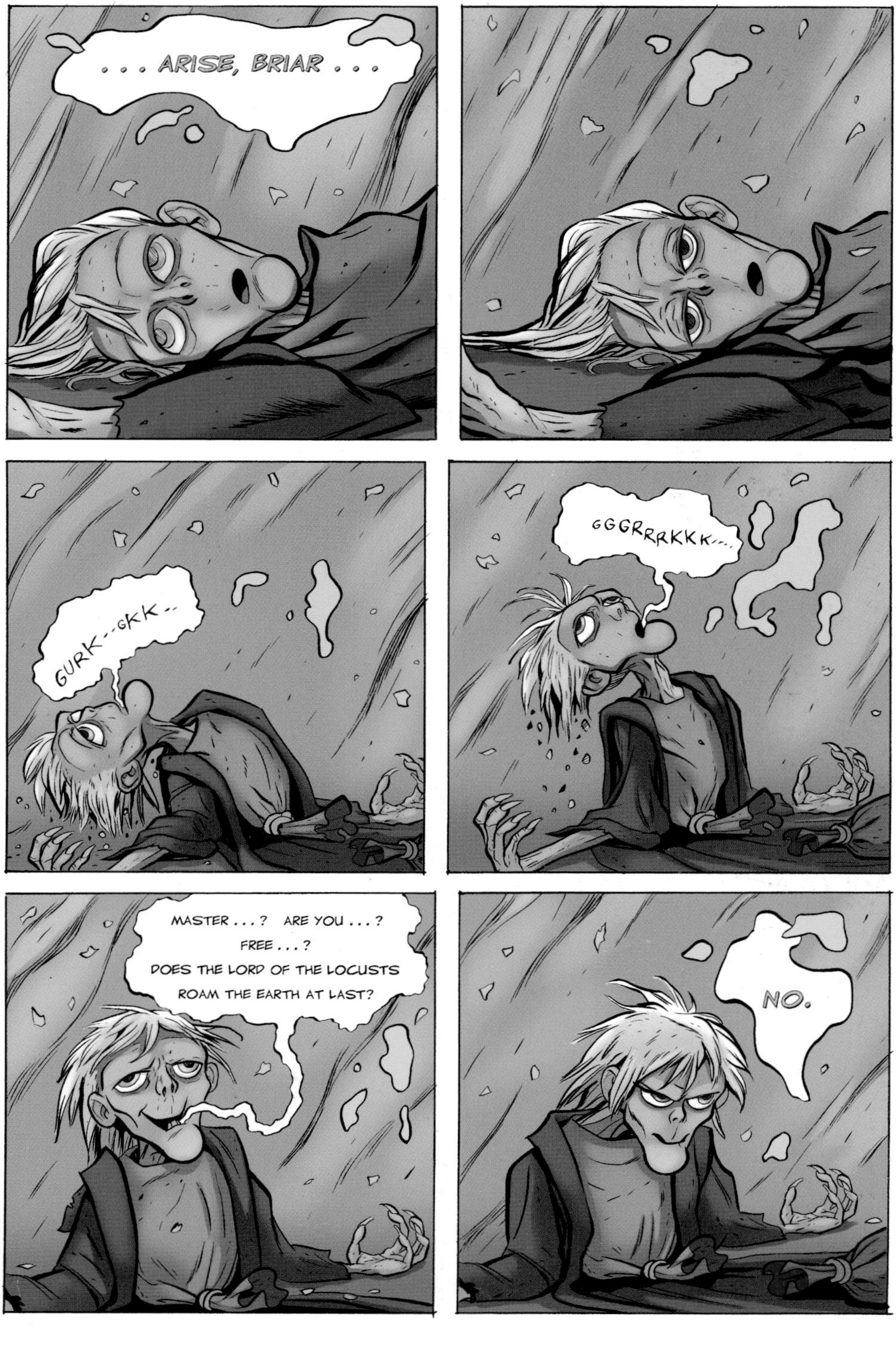
. . . ARISE, BRIAR . . .
GURK--GKK--
GGGRRRKKK....
MASTER . . . ? ARE YOU . . . ?
FREE . . . ?
DOES THE LORD OF THE LOCUSTS
ROAM THE EARTH AT LAST?
NO.

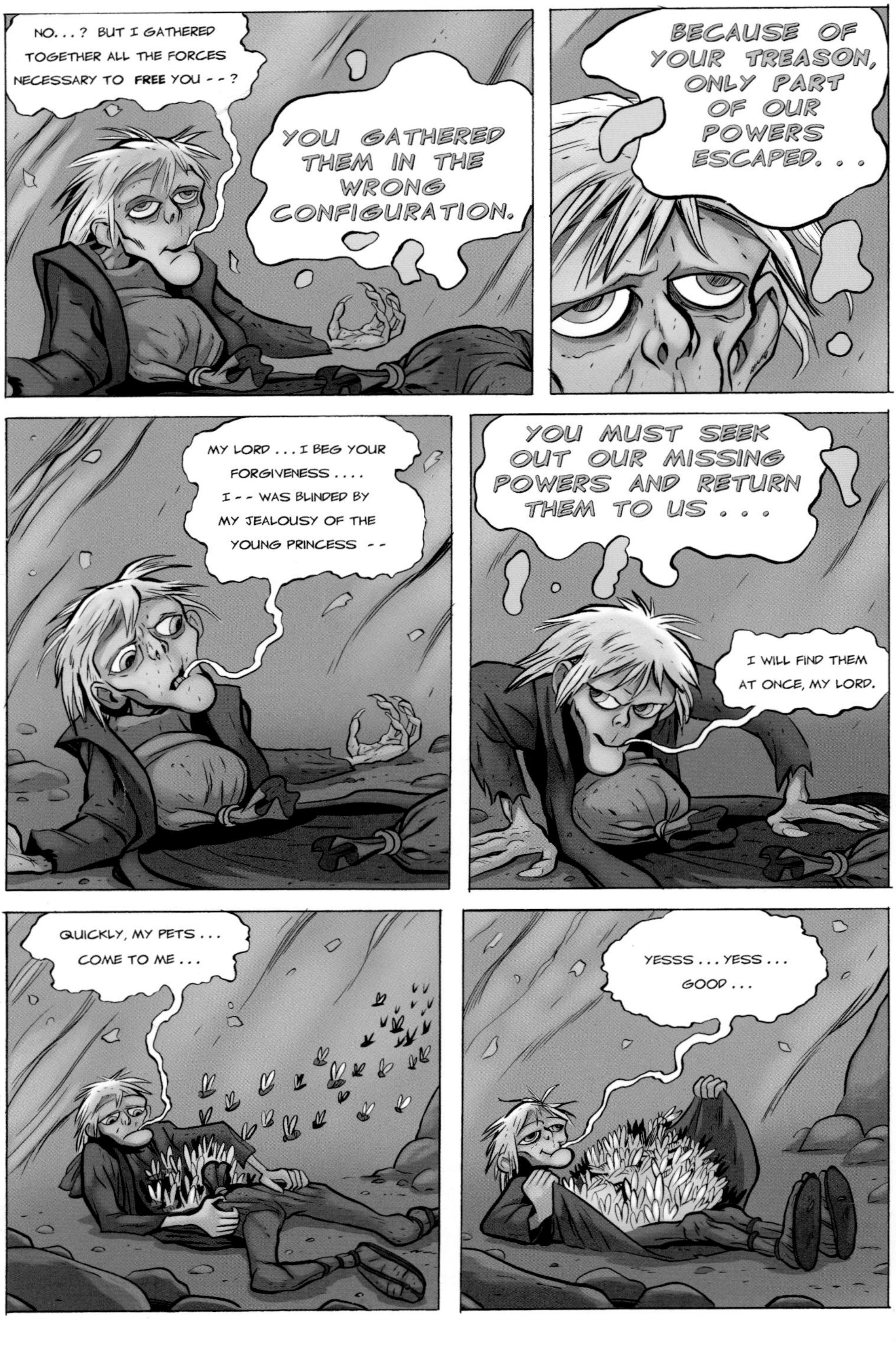
NO. . . ? BUT I GATHERED TOGETHER ALL THE FORCES NECESSARY TO FREE YOU - - ?
YOU GATHERED THEM IN THE WRONG CONFIGURATION.
BECAUSE OF YOUR TREASON, ONLY PART OF OUR POWERS ESCAPED. . .
MY LORD . . . I BEG YOUR FORGIVENESS . . . . I - - WAS BLINDED BY MY JEALOUSY OF THE YOUNG PRINCESS - -
YOU MUST SEEK OUT OUR MISSING POWERS AND RETURN THEM TO US . . .
I WILL FIND THEM AT ONCE, MY LORD.
QUICKLY, MY PETS . . . COME TO ME . . .
YESSS . . . YESS . . . GOOD . . .

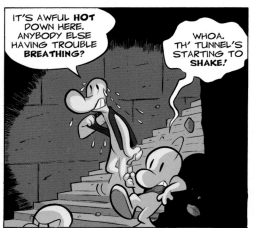

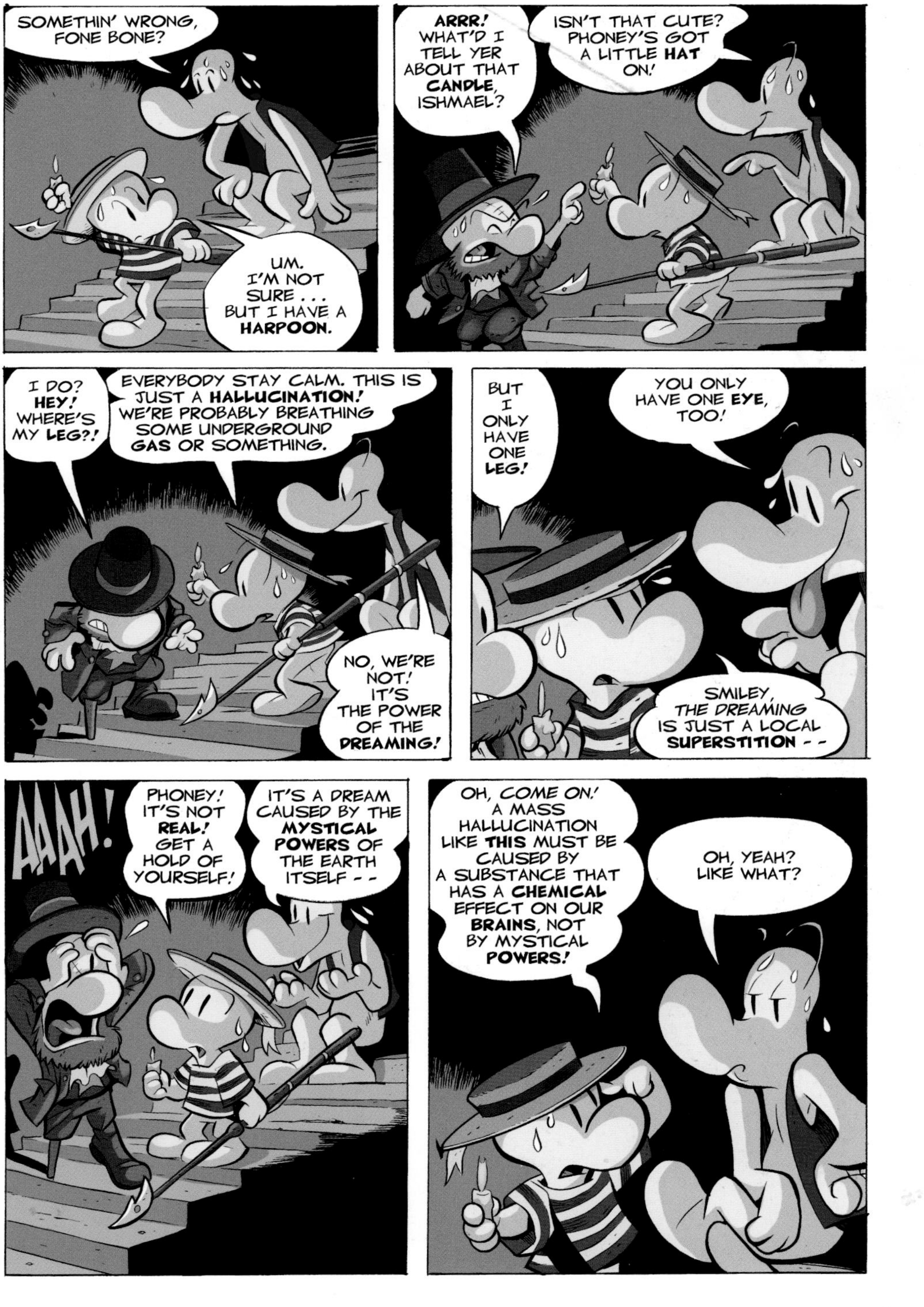
SOMETHIN' WRONG, FONE BONE?
UM. I'M NOT SURE . . . BUT I HAVE A HARPOON.
ARRR! WHAT'D I TELL YER ABOUT THAT CANDLE, ISHMAEL?
ISN'T THAT CUTE? PHONEY'S GOT A LITTLE HAT ON!
I DO? HEY! WHERE'S MY LEG?!
EVERYBODY STAY CALM. THIS IS JUST A HALLUCINATION! WE'RE PROBABLY BREATHING SOME UNDERGROUND GAS OR SOMETHING.
NO, WE'RE NOT! IT'S THE POWER OF THE DREAMING!
BUT I ONLY HAVE ONE LEG!
YOU ONLY HAVE ONE EYE, TOO!
SMILEY, THE DREAMING IS JUST A LOCAL SUPERSTITION - -
AAAH!
PHONEY! IT'S NOT REAL! GET A HOLD OF YOURSELF!
IT'S A DREAM CAUSED BY THE MYSTICAL POWERS OF THE EARTH ITSELF - -
OH, COME ON! A MASS HALLUCINATION LIKE THIS MUST BE CAUSED BY A SUBSTANCE THAT HAS A CHEMICAL EFFECT ON OUR BRAINS, NOT BY MYSTICAL POWERS!
OH, YEAH? LIKE WHAT?

LIKE AN INVISIBLE GAS!

MYSTICAL POWERS . . . INVISIBLE GAS . . . SEEMS TO ME LIKE YOU'RE SPLITTING HAIRS.

BUT IF IT **IS** GAS, DON'T YOU THINK YOU SHOULD DOUSE THAT OPEN **FLAME?**

OHMYGOSH! YOU'RE **RIGHT!**

PSSSS

UNN---

GRAN'MA! WHAT HAPPENED?

THORN JUST COLLAPSED! AND SHE'S ICE COLD.

ICE COLD?! IT'S A BILLION DEGREES IN HERE!

DID SHE SUCCUMB TO THE GAS?

I THINK IT'S THE LOCUSTS.

COME HERE, EVERYONE. . . GET CLOSE! TRY TO KEEP HER WARM.

WHAT DO YOU MEAN THE LOCUSTS?

WHAT DID THEY DO TO HER?

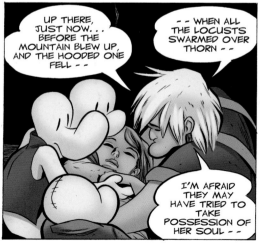

UP THERE, JUST NOW. . . BEFORE THE MOUNTAIN BLEW UP, AND THE HOODED ONE FELL - -

- - WHEN ALL THE LOCUSTS SWARMED OVER THORN - -

I'M AFRAID THEY MAY HAVE TRIED TO TAKE POSSESSION OF HER SOUL - -

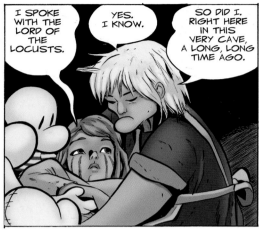

THORN, ARE YOU **SURE** YOU'RE OKAY?

YES. BUT I'M WORRIED ABOUT THE VALLEY. WE NEED TO GET OUT OF THIS CAVE.

THERE'S LIGHT COMING FROM UP AHEAD. . .

SO TELL ME, GRAN'MA, WHO ELSE HAS A DREAMING EYE BESIDES YOU AND ME?

WHY, EVERYONE HAS ONE, DEAR . . .

SOME ARE MORE OPEN THAN OTHERS, BUT IT'S THE PLACE WHERE THE DREAMING FLOWS THROUGH YOU.

SO YOU KNEW HOW POWERFUL BRIAR'S EYE WAS.

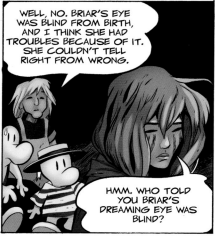

WELL, NO. BRIAR'S EYE WAS BLIND FROM BIRTH, AND I THINK SHE HAD TROUBLES BECAUSE OF IT. SHE COULDN'T TELL RIGHT FROM WRONG.

HMM. WHO TOLD YOU BRIAR'S DREAMING EYE WAS BLIND?

BRIAR DID.

IT WASN'T TRUE?

NO. AND NOT ONLY WAS BRIAR'S DREAMING EYE NEVER BLIND, IF I'M NOT MISTAKEN, IT'S **STILL OPEN!**

HEY! THE GATE'S THIS WAY!

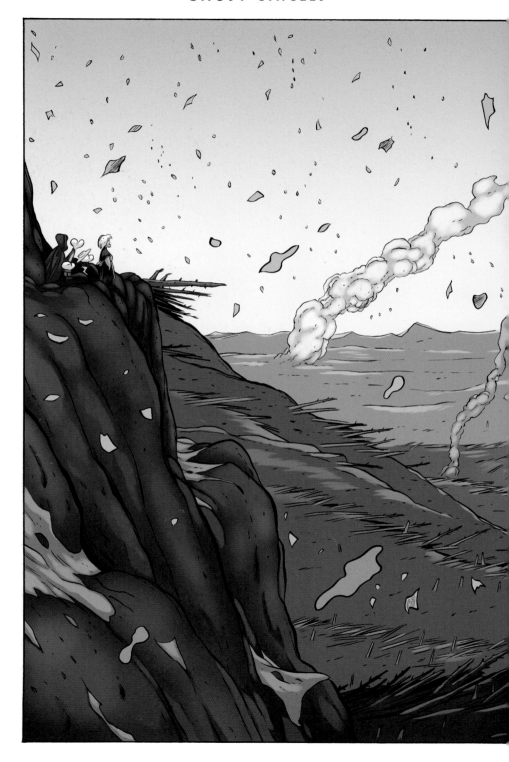

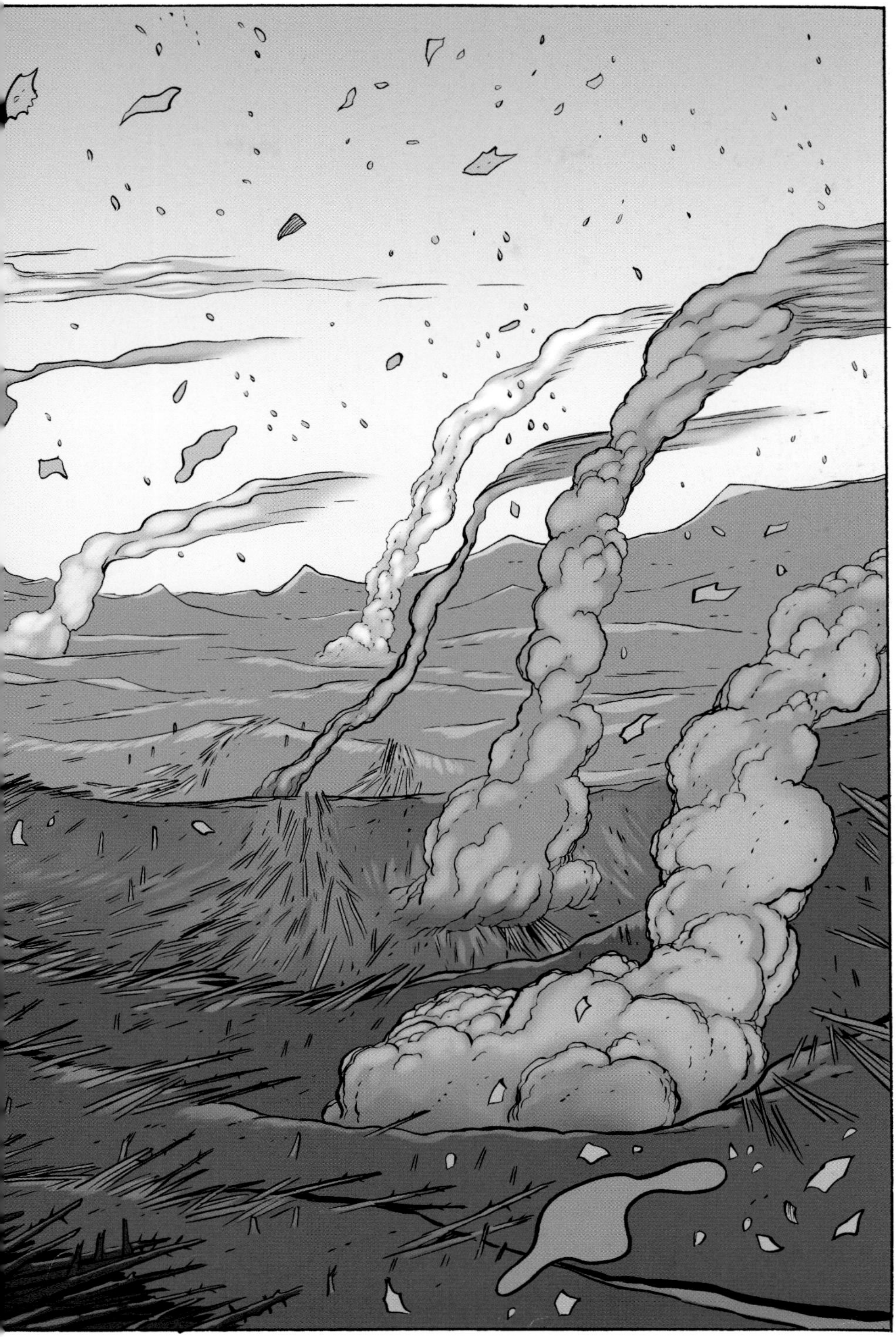

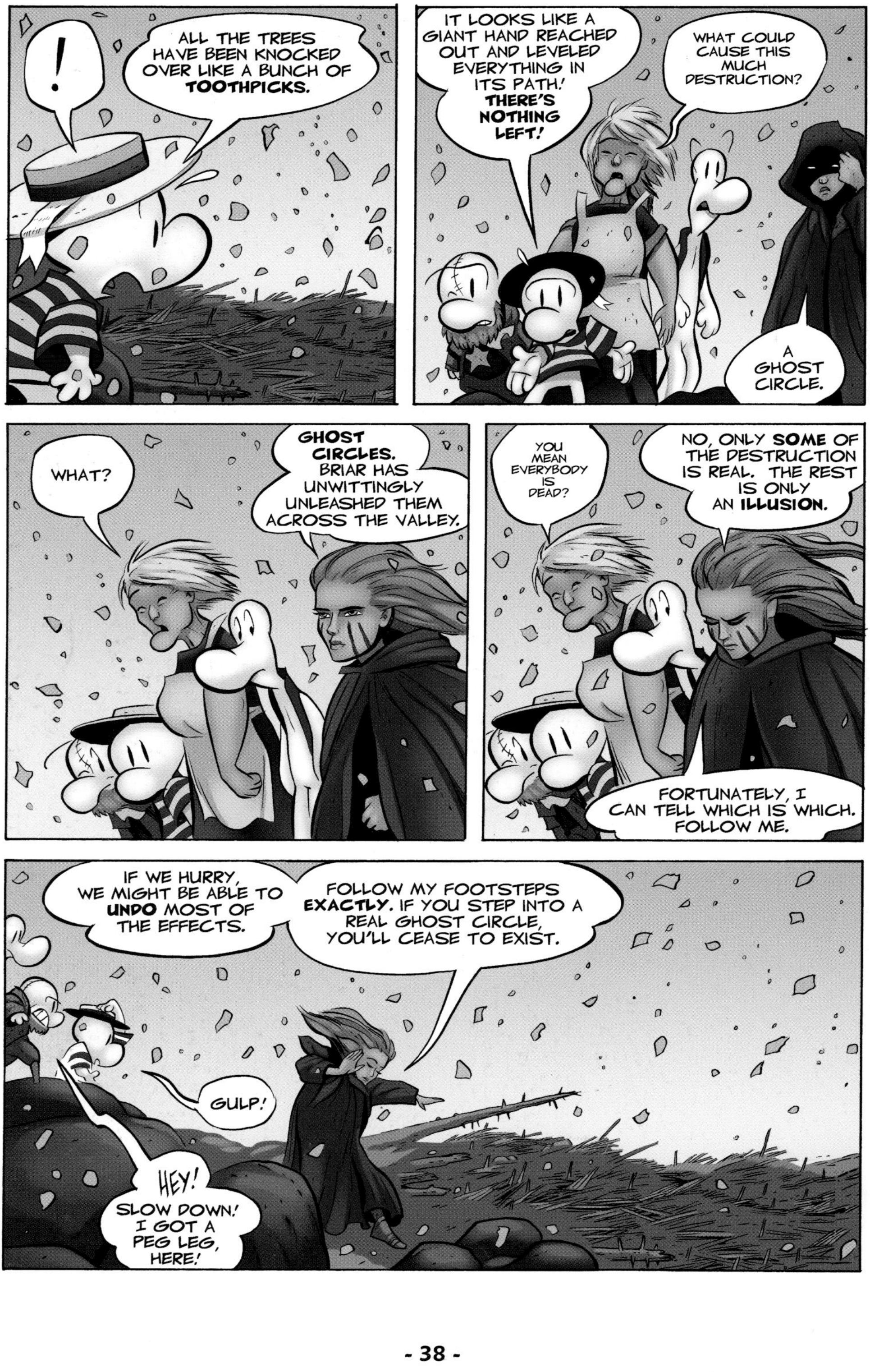
!
ALL THE TREES HAVE BEEN KNOCKED OVER LIKE A BUNCH OF **TOOTHPICKS.**
IT LOOKS LIKE A GIANT HAND REACHED OUT AND LEVELED EVERYTHING IN ITS PATH! **THERE'S NOTHING LEFT!**
WHAT COULD CAUSE THIS MUCH DESTRUCTION?
A GHOST CIRCLE.
WHAT?
GHOST CIRCLES. BRIAR HAS UNWITTINGLY UNLEASHED THEM ACROSS THE VALLEY.
YOU MEAN EVERYBODY IS DEAD?
NO, ONLY **SOME** OF THE DESTRUCTION IS REAL. THE REST IS ONLY AN **ILLUSION.**
FORTUNATELY, I CAN TELL WHICH IS WHICH. FOLLOW ME.
IF WE HURRY, WE MIGHT BE ABLE TO **UNDO** MOST OF THE EFFECTS.
FOLLOW MY FOOTSTEPS **EXACTLY.** IF YOU STEP INTO A REAL GHOST CIRCLE, YOU'LL CEASE TO EXIST.
GULP!
HEY!
SLOW DOWN! I GOT A PEG LEG, HERE!

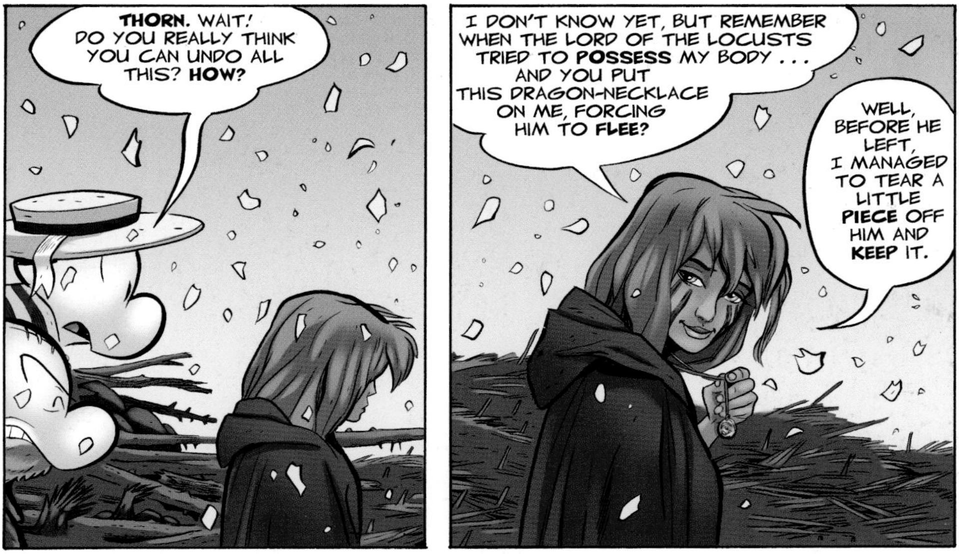
THORN. WAIT! DO YOU REALLY THINK YOU CAN UNDO ALL THIS? HOW?
I DON'T KNOW YET, BUT REMEMBER WHEN THE LORD OF THE LOCUSTS TRIED TO POSSESS MY BODY . . . AND YOU PUT THIS DRAGON-NECKLACE ON ME, FORCING HIM TO FLEE?
WELL, BEFORE HE LEFT, I MANAGED TO TEAR A LITTLE PIECE OFF HIM AND KEEP IT.

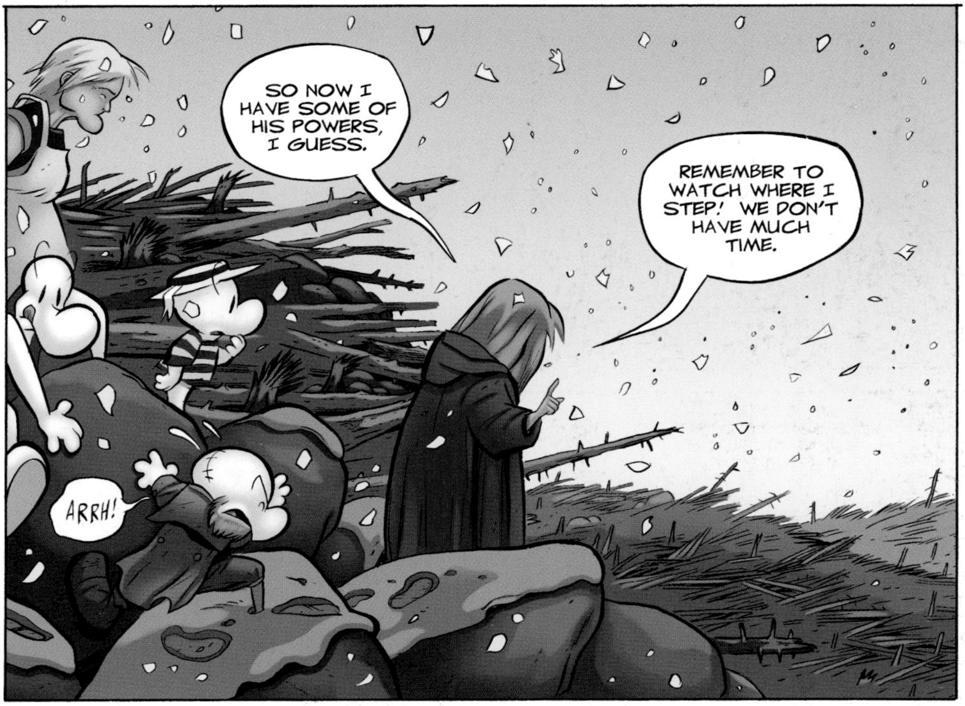
SO NOW I HAVE SOME OF HIS POWERS, I GUESS.
REMEMBER TO WATCH WHERE I STEP! WE DON'T HAVE MUCH TIME.
ARRH!

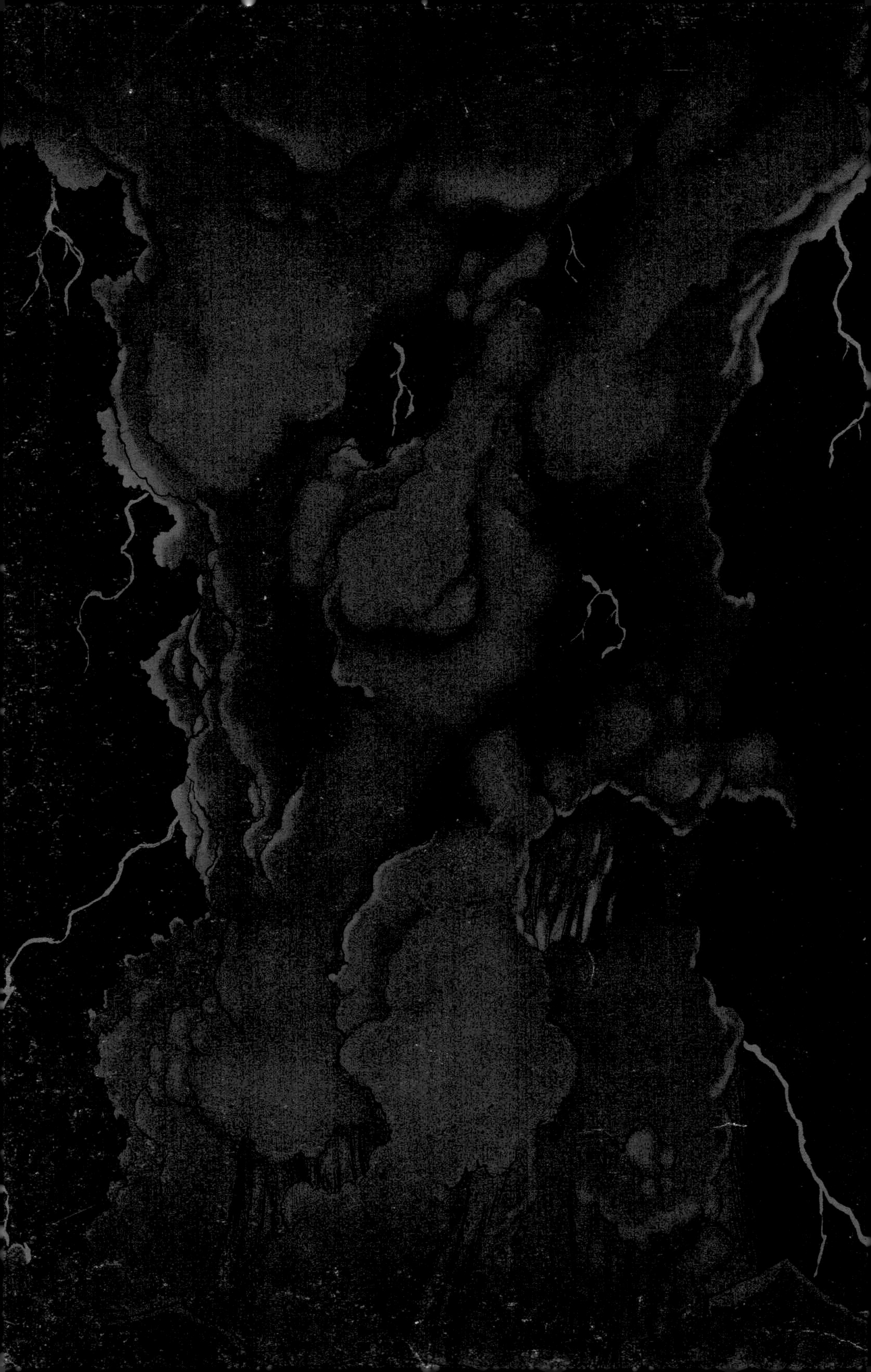

I'M NOT LETTING THEM GET TO ME. I'M AS SKEPTICAL ABOUT ALL THIS **DREAM** STUFF AS YOU ARE...

BUT UNTIL I HAVE **SOME** EXPLANATION FOR WHY YOU AND I ARE DRESSED LIKE CHARACTERS OUT OF MY **MOBY DICK** DREAM, I'M GOING TO PROCEED WITH **CAUTION**, OKAY?

C'MON, GUYS, CUT IT OUT. I DON'T LIKE IT WHEN YOU FIGHT.

WHAT ARE TALKING ABOUT? YOU **LOVE** IT WHEN WE FIGHT!

THIS IS DIFFERENT. I'M **THIRSTY**.

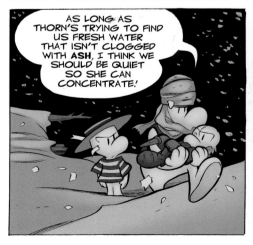

AS LONG AS THORN'S TRYING TO FIND US FRESH WATER THAT ISN'T CLOGGED WITH **ASH**, I THINK WE SHOULD BE QUIET SO SHE CAN CONCENTRATE!

WAIT...

THE WAY AHEAD IS NARROW-- WATCH MY FOOTSTEPS CAREFULLY--

AND THAT ROCK IS OFF-LIMITS.

JEEZ!

BE CAREFUL YOU LUNKHEAD, MY PEG LEG ALMOST TOUCHED THE ROCK.

RRR.

WE NEED TO STOP. I'M GETTING TIRED.

HOW CAN YOU BE TIRED?!! YOU'RE BEING CARRIED!

DO YOU EVER THINK ABOUT ANYTHING OTHER THAN YOURSELF?!

WHAT ABOUT THE REST OF US WHO ARE JUST TRYING TO SURVIVE THE MESS YOU MADE?!

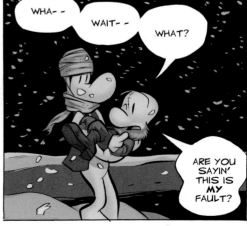

WHA--

WAIT--

WHAT?

ARE YOU SAYIN' THIS IS MY FAULT?

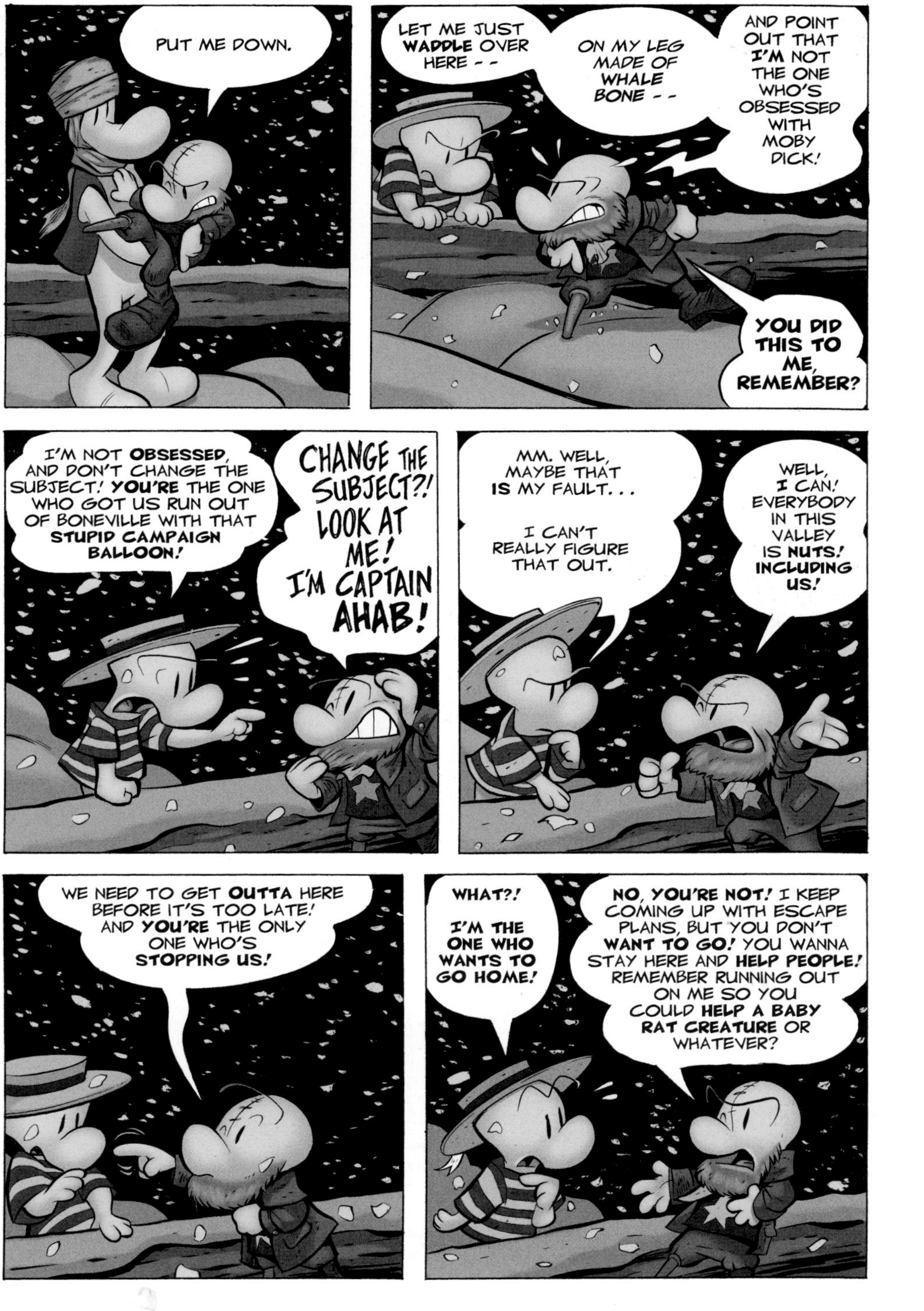
PUT ME DOWN.
LET ME JUST WADDLE OVER HERE - -
ON MY LEG MADE OF WHALE BONE - -
AND POINT OUT THAT I'M NOT THE ONE WHO'S OBSESSED WITH MOBY DICK!
YOU DID THIS TO ME, REMEMBER?
I'M NOT OBSESSED, AND DON'T CHANGE THE SUBJECT! YOU'RE THE ONE WHO GOT US RUN OUT OF BONEVILLE WITH THAT STUPID CAMPAIGN BALLOON!
CHANGE THE SUBJECT?! LOOK AT ME! I'M CAPTAIN AHAB!
MM. WELL, MAYBE THAT IS MY FAULT...
I CAN'T REALLY FIGURE THAT OUT.
WELL, I CAN! EVERYBODY IN THIS VALLEY IS NUTS! INCLUDING US!
WE NEED TO GET OUTTA HERE BEFORE IT'S TOO LATE! AND YOU'RE THE ONLY ONE WHO'S STOPPING US!
WHAT?!
I'M THE ONE WHO WANTS TO GO HOME!
NO, YOU'RE NOT! I KEEP COMING UP WITH ESCAPE PLANS, BUT YOU DON'T WANT TO GO! YOU WANNA STAY HERE AND HELP PEOPLE! REMEMBER RUNNING OUT ON ME SO YOU COULD HELP A BABY RAT CREATURE OR WHATEVER?

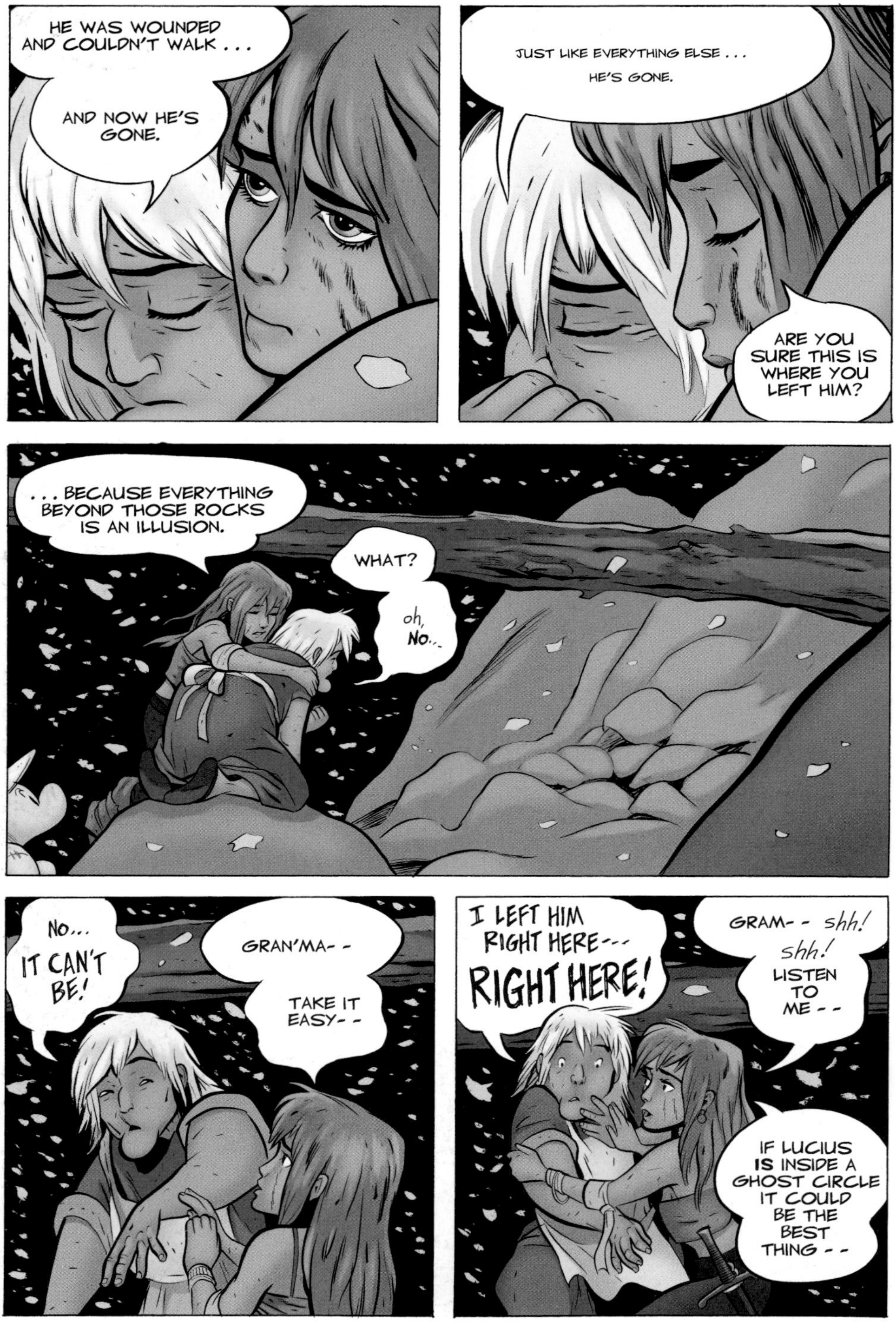
HE WAS WOUNDED AND COULDN'T WALK . . .
AND NOW HE'S GONE.
JUST LIKE EVERYTHING ELSE . . .
HE'S GONE.
ARE YOU SURE THIS IS WHERE YOU LEFT HIM?
. . . BECAUSE EVERYTHING BEYOND THOSE ROCKS IS AN ILLUSION.
WHAT?
oh, NO...
NO... IT CAN'T BE!
GRAN'MA- -
TAKE IT EASY- -
I LEFT HIM RIGHT HERE--- RIGHT HERE!
GRAM- - shh! shh!
LISTEN TO ME - -
IF LUCIUS IS INSIDE A GHOST CIRCLE IT COULD BE THE BEST THING - -

- - IF HE'D BEEN IN THE PATH OF THE TRUE BLAST, HE WOULD HAVE BEEN KILLED FOR CERTAIN - -

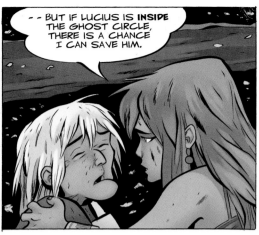

- - BUT IF LUCIUS IS **INSIDE** THE GHOST CIRCLE, THERE IS A CHANCE I CAN SAVE HIM.

I MIGHT BE ABLE TO **UNDO** THE SPELL WITH THE PIECE OF THE LOCUST THAT I HAVE INSIDE OF ME.

OH, THORN . . .

WHAT'S HAPPENED TO YOU - - . . .WHAT'S HAPPENED TO THE WORLD?

I DIDN'T KNOW THIS COULD HAPPEN. . . I - -

WELL? IS HE IN THERE?

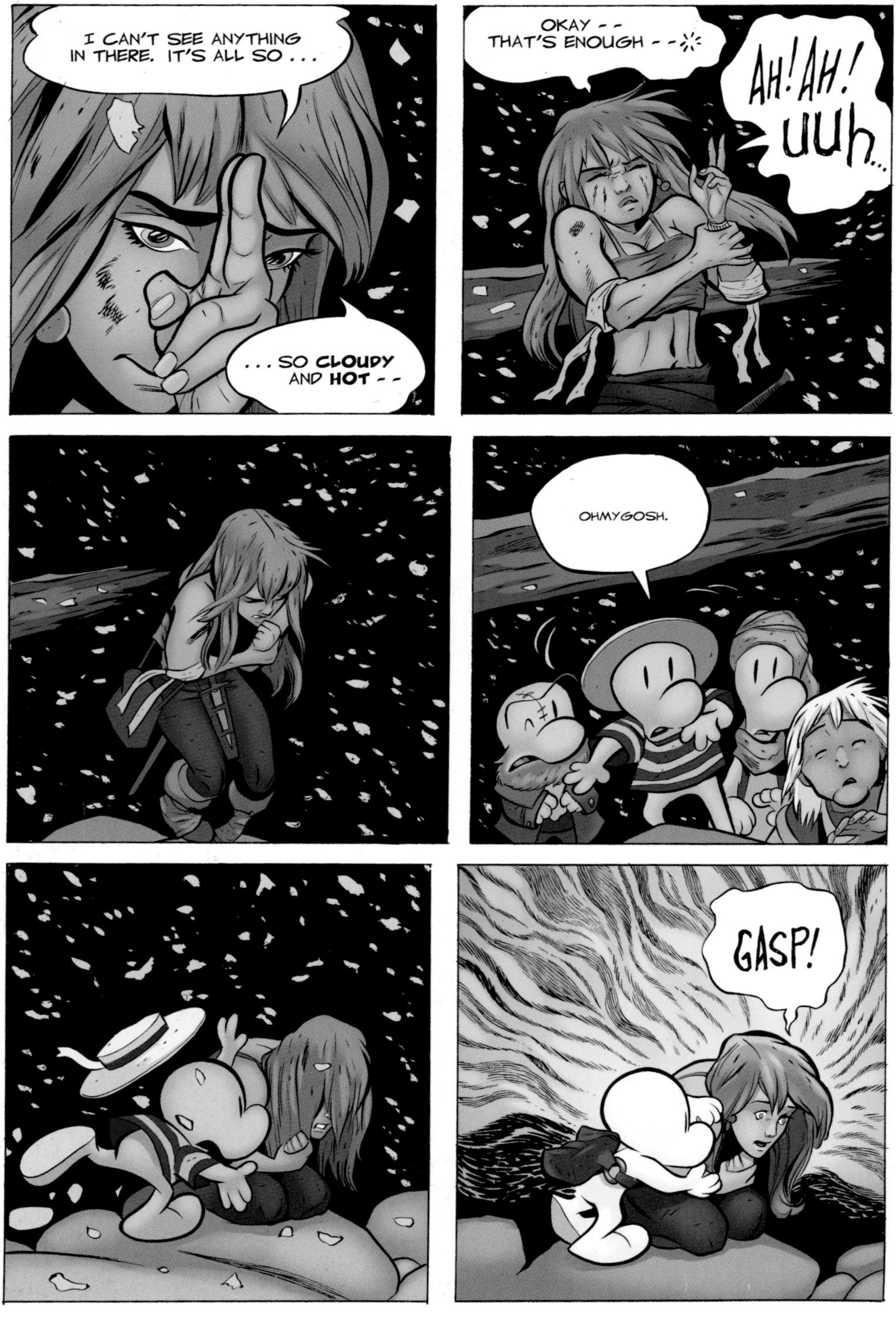
I CAN'T SEE ANYTHING IN THERE. IT'S ALL SO . . .
. . . SO CLOUDY AND HOT - -
OKAY - - THAT'S ENOUGH - -
AH! AH! uuh...
OHMYGOSH.
GASP!

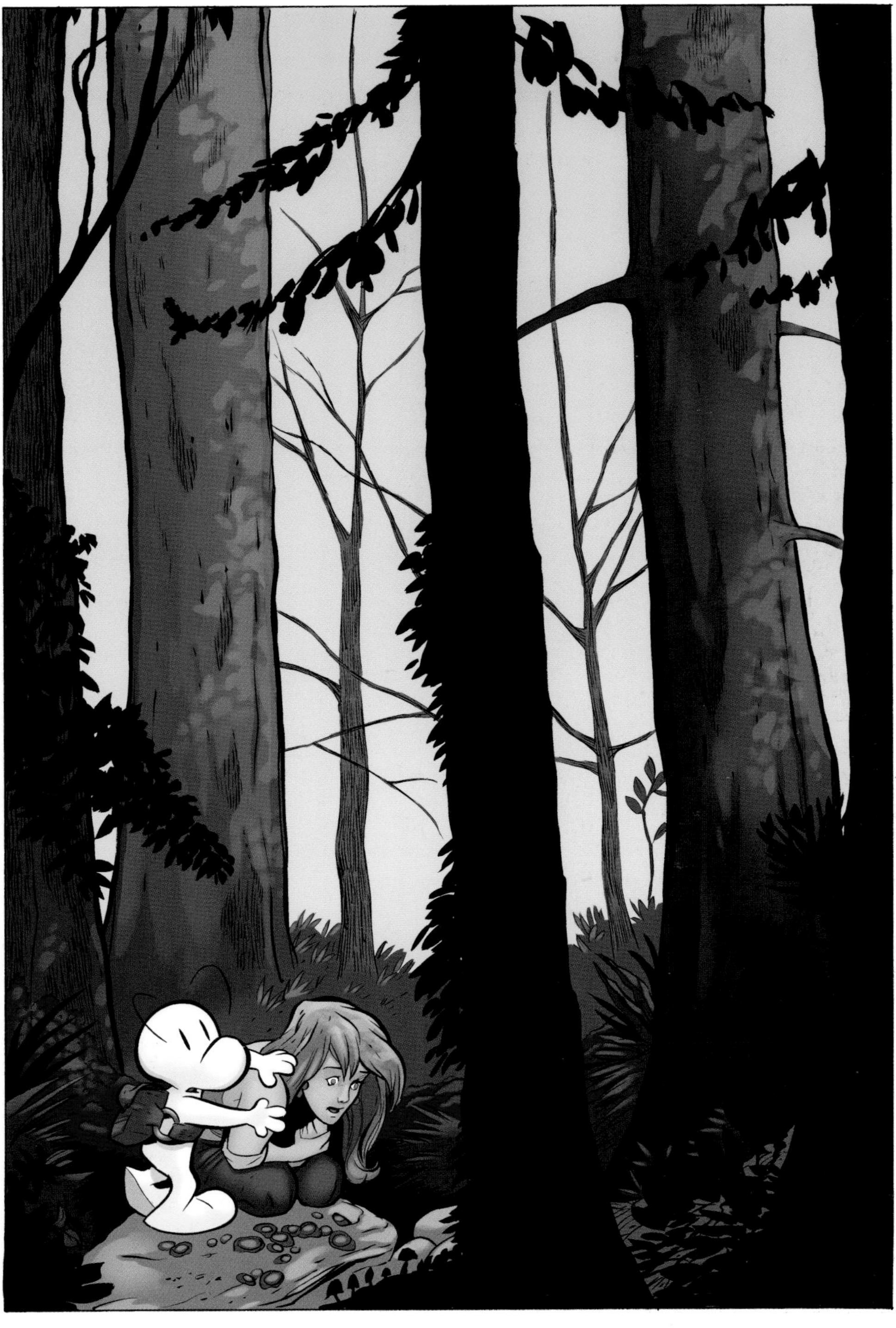

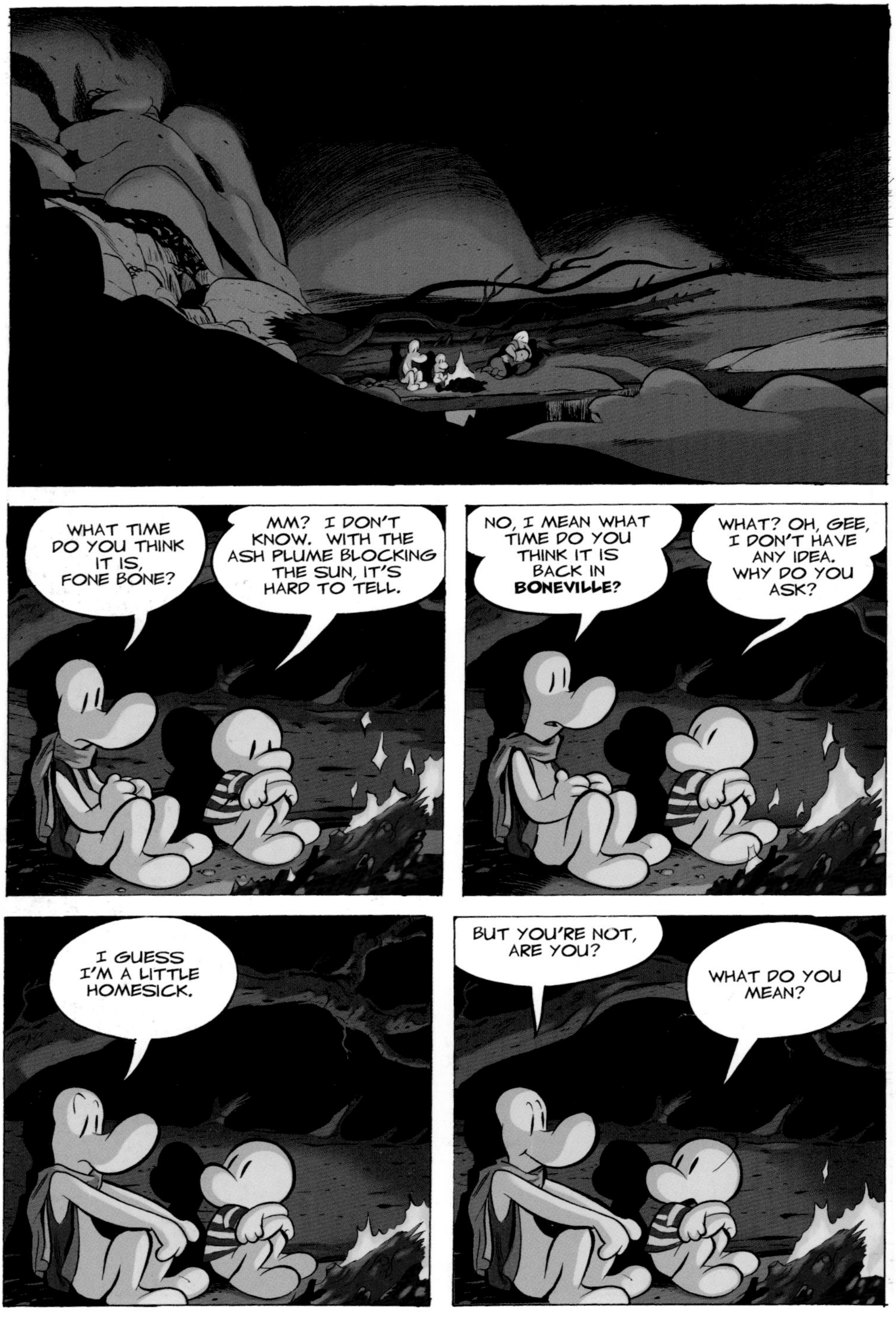
WHAT TIME DO YOU THINK IT IS, FONE BONE?
MM? I DON'T KNOW. WITH THE ASH PLUME BLOCKING THE SUN, IT'S HARD TO TELL.
NO, I MEAN WHAT TIME DO YOU THINK IT IS BACK IN BONEVILLE?
WHAT? OH, GEE, I DON'T HAVE ANY IDEA. WHY DO YOU ASK?
I GUESS I'M A LITTLE HOMESICK.
BUT YOU'RE NOT, ARE YOU?
WHAT DO YOU MEAN?

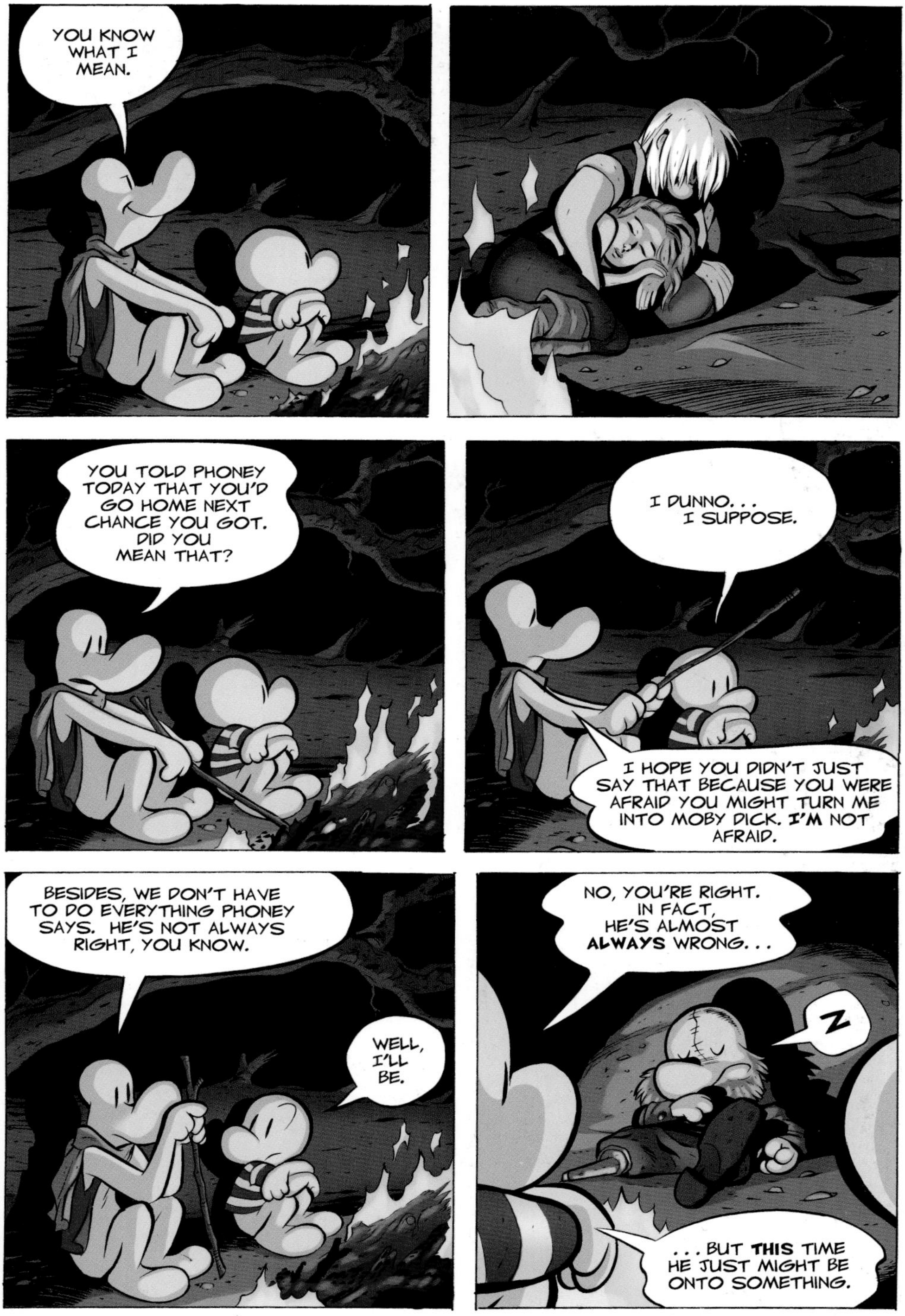
YOU KNOW WHAT I MEAN.
YOU TOLD PHONEY TODAY THAT YOU'D GO HOME NEXT CHANCE YOU GOT. DID YOU MEAN THAT?
I DUNNO. . . I SUPPOSE.
I HOPE YOU DIDN'T JUST SAY THAT BECAUSE YOU WERE AFRAID YOU MIGHT TURN ME INTO MOBY DICK. I'M NOT AFRAID.
BESIDES, WE DON'T HAVE TO DO EVERYTHING PHONEY SAYS. HE'S NOT ALWAYS RIGHT, YOU KNOW.
WELL, I'LL BE.
NO, YOU'RE RIGHT. IN FACT, HE'S ALMOST ALWAYS WRONG. . .
Z
. . . BUT THIS TIME HE JUST MIGHT BE ONTO SOMETHING.

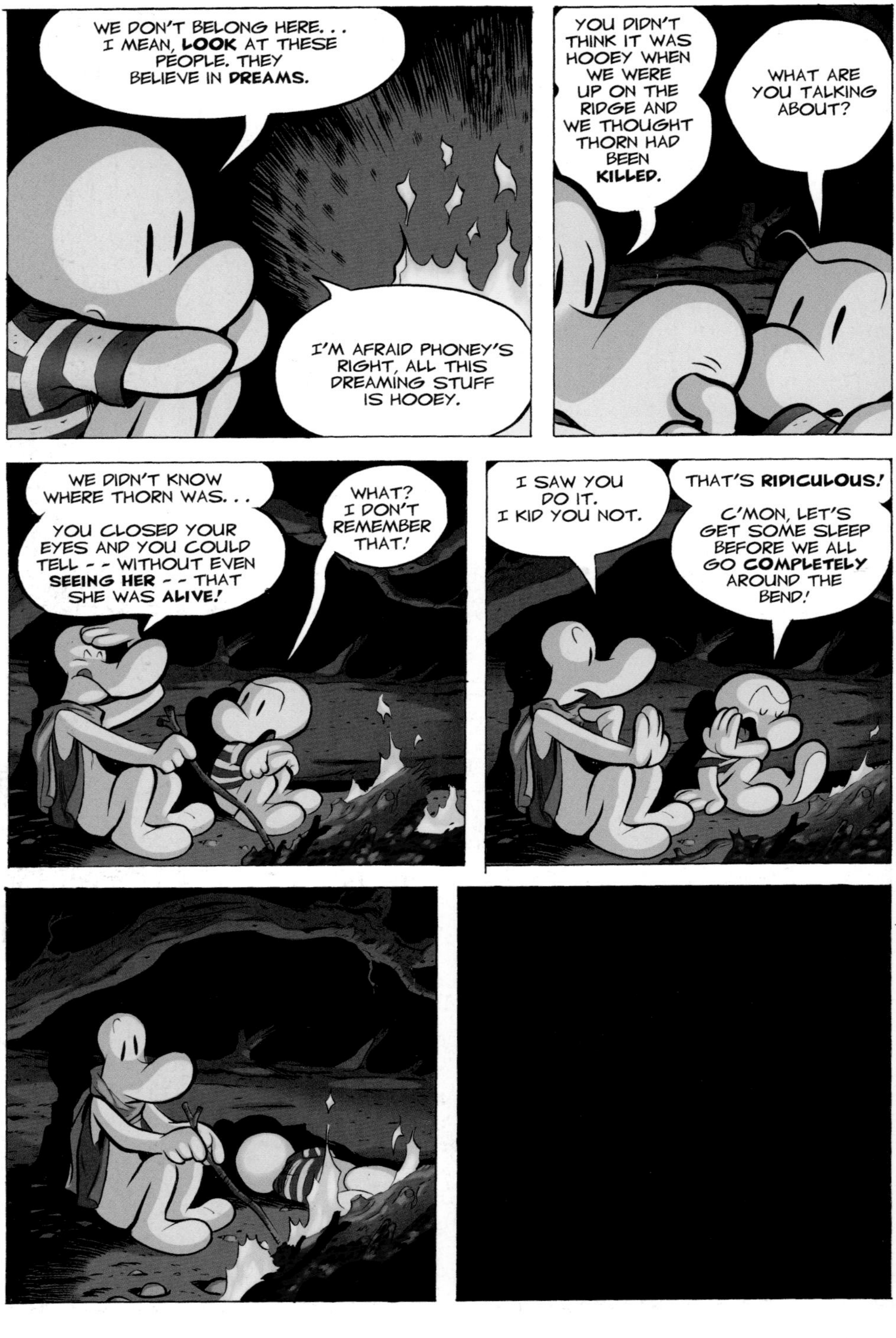
WE DON'T BELONG HERE... I MEAN, LOOK AT THESE PEOPLE. THEY BELIEVE IN DREAMS.
I'M AFRAID PHONEY'S RIGHT, ALL THIS DREAMING STUFF IS HOOEY.
YOU DIDN'T THINK IT WAS HOOEY WHEN WE WERE UP ON THE RIDGE AND WE THOUGHT THORN HAD BEEN KILLED.
WHAT ARE YOU TALKING ABOUT?
WE DIDN'T KNOW WHERE THORN WAS...
YOU CLOSED YOUR EYES AND YOU COULD TELL -- WITHOUT EVEN SEEING HER -- THAT SHE WAS ALIVE!
WHAT? I DON'T REMEMBER THAT!
I SAW YOU DO IT. I KID YOU NOT.
THAT'S RIDICULOUS!
C'MON, LET'S GET SOME SLEEP BEFORE WE ALL GO COMPLETELY AROUND THE BEND!

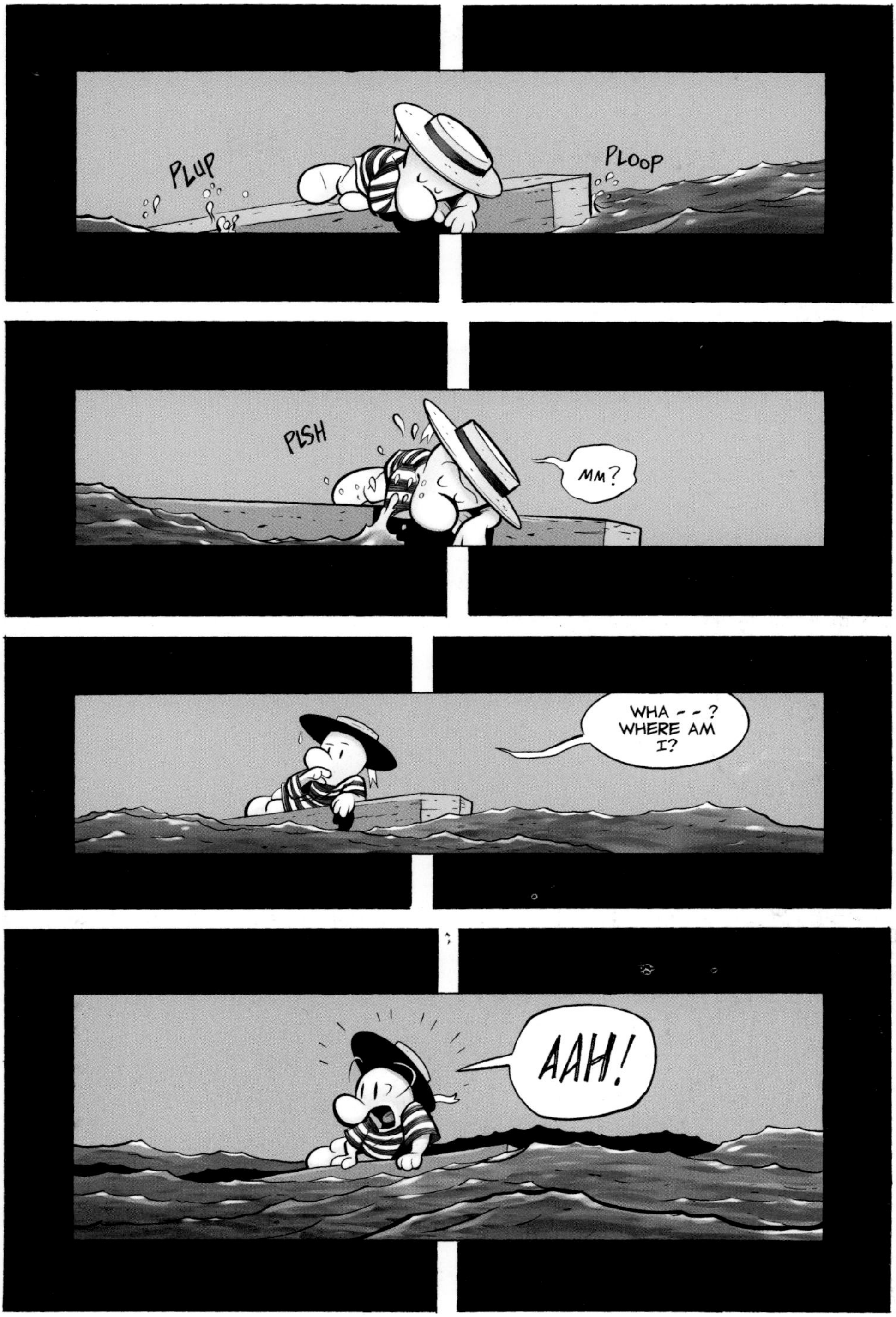
PLUP
PLOOP
PLSH
MM?
WHA - - ? WHERE AM I?
AAH!

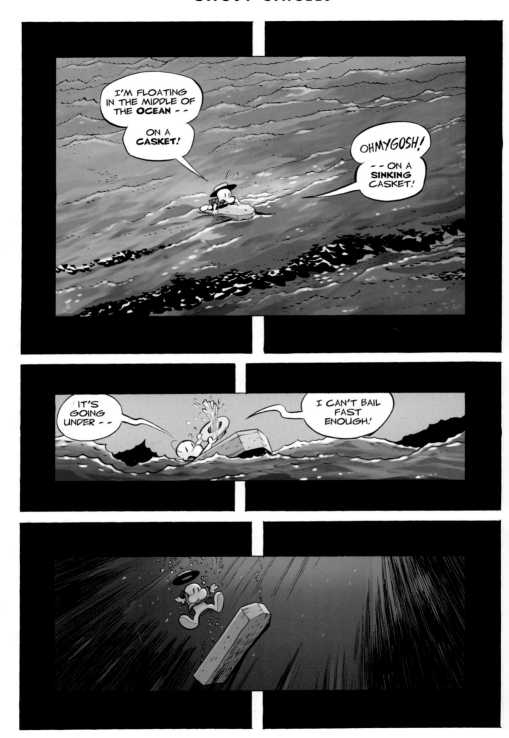

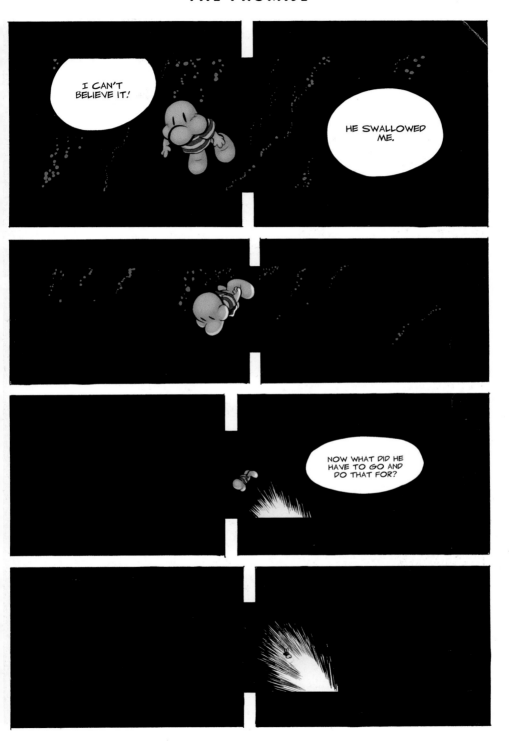

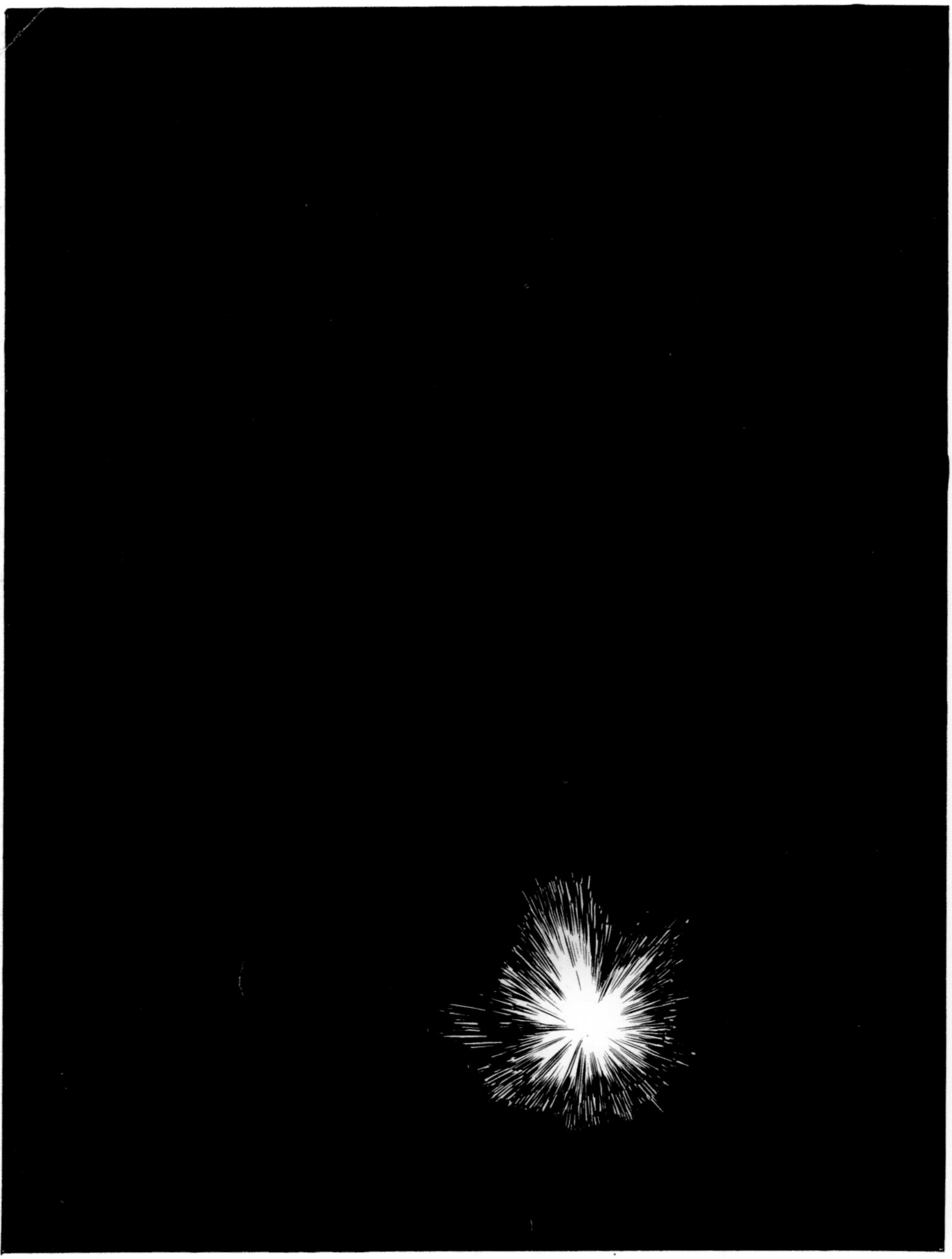

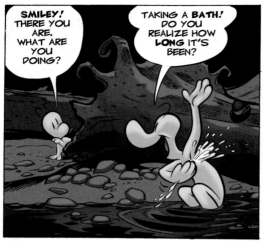

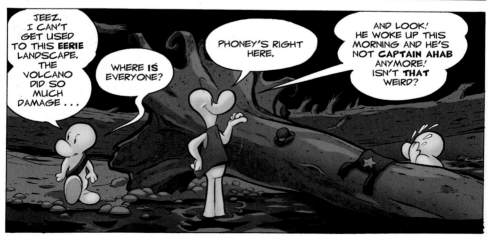

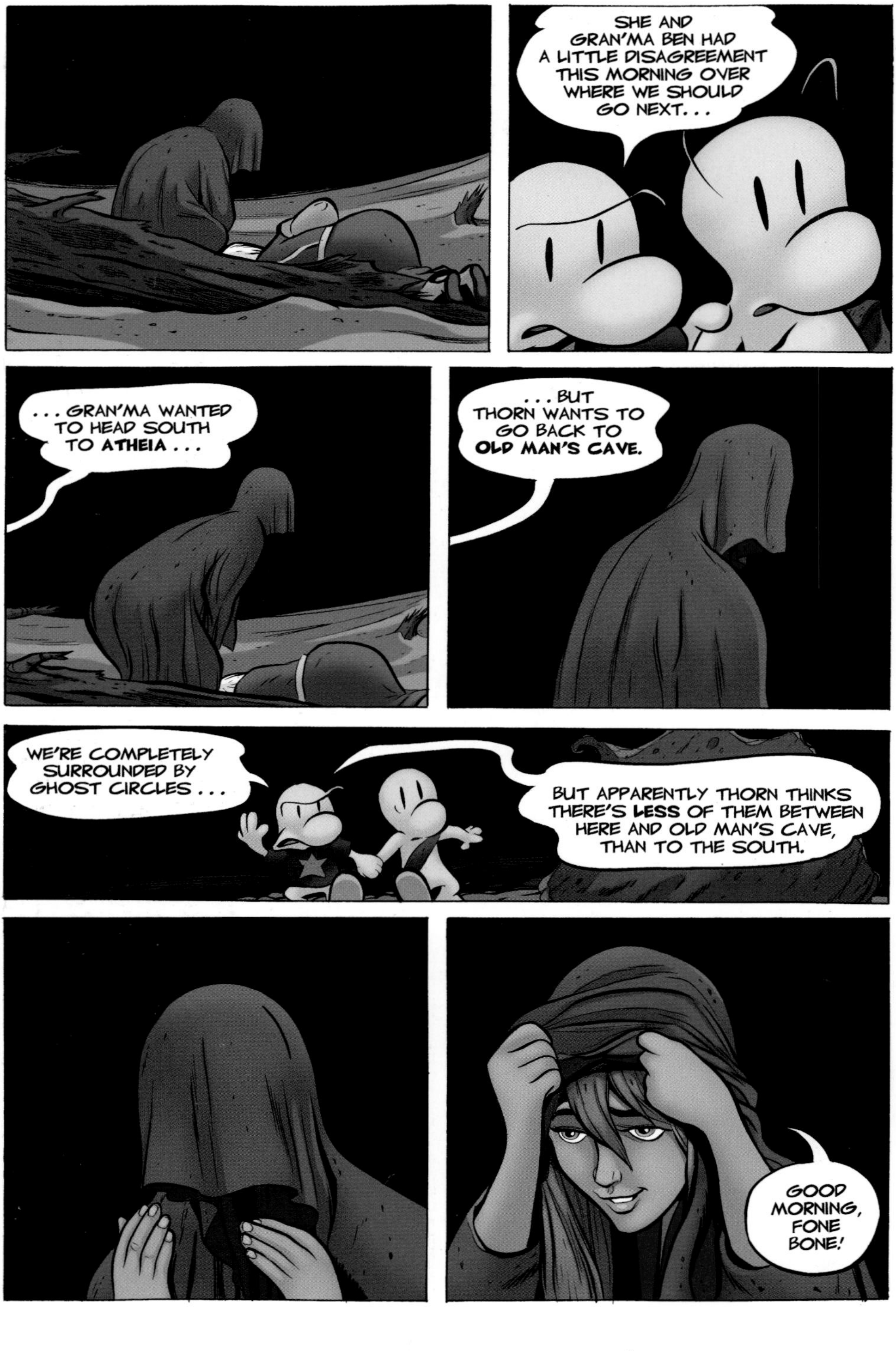
SHE AND GRAN'MA BEN HAD A LITTLE DISAGREEMENT THIS MORNING OVER WHERE WE SHOULD GO NEXT. . .
. . . GRAN'MA WANTED TO HEAD SOUTH TO ATHEIA . . .
. . . BUT THORN WANTS TO GO BACK TO OLD MAN'S CAVE.
WE'RE COMPLETELY SURROUNDED BY GHOST CIRCLES . . .
BUT APPARENTLY THORN THINKS THERE'S LESS OF THEM BETWEEN HERE AND OLD MAN'S CAVE, THAN TO THE SOUTH.
GOOD MORNING, FONE BONE!

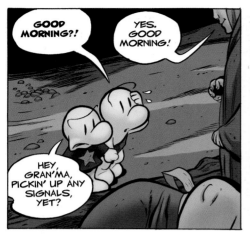

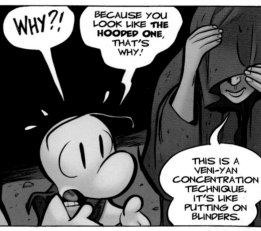

HAVE YOU FOUND THE OUTER EDGE OF THE CIRCLES, THORN?

NOT YET. I THINK THE GHOST CIRCLES MAY BE **SPREADING.**

WHAT?!

THE EXPLOSION FROM THE VOLCANO PUSHED THEM TO THE FAR CORNERS OF THE VALLEY...

...BUT EVEN THOUGH THE BLAST **ITSELF** HAS DISSIPATED, THE CIRCLES CONTINUE TO SPREAD OUTWARD.

OH, BROTHER, HERE WE GO... SO **YOU'RE** TELLIN' US THAT TH' **GHOST CIRCLES** AREN'T PART OF THE NATURAL VOLCANO - - THEY'RE SOMETHING **SEPARATE** - -

SOMETHING **EVIL!**

NOT SEPARATE. PART OF THE **DREAMING,** LIKE EVERYTHING ELSE...

BUT FROM A **PART** OF THE DREAMING WHERE THERE IS NO **SHAPE** OR **FORM.** ONLY **VOID** AND **NOTHINGNESS.**

DURING THE CEREMONY WHEN THE HOODED ONE ATTEMPTED TO **FREE** THE LOCUST- - THE NOTHINGNESS BEGAN TO COME HERE ...

FORTUNATELY FOR US, THE HOODED ONE **BOTCHED** THE RITUAL AND ONLY THE SMALLEST FRACTION OF THE VOID WAS ABLE TO ESCAPE.

THAT'S WHAT THE GHOST CIRCLES ARE - - PLACES WHERE **OUR** WORLD AND THE VOID ARE **MIXED TOGETHER.**

YOU CALL THAT **FORTUNATE?**

IF THE CEREMONY HAD BEEN **SUCCESSFUL,** NOT ONLY WOULD I **BE** THE LORD OF THE LOCUSTS, BUT THE ENTIRE **VALLEY** WOULD BE A GHOSTLY **NETHER-WORLD.**

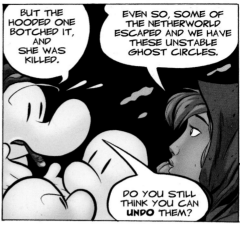

BUT THE HOODED ONE BOTCHED IT, AND SHE WAS KILLED.

EVEN SO, SOME OF THE NETHERWORLD ESCAPED AND WE HAVE THESE UNSTABLE GHOST CIRCLES.

DO YOU STILL THINK YOU CAN **UNDO** THEM?

WELL, IT **FEELS** LIKE THE ONLY THING HOLDING THE CIRCLES HERE IS THE SMALL PIECE OF THE LOCUST THAT'S INSIDE ME. . .

I SAY THIS IS ALL **HOOEY!** WE'RE JUST **HALLUCINATING!**

SHUT UP, PHONEY! HOW DO WE GET RID OF THAT PIECE THAT'S INSIDE YOU?

GRAN'MA BEN THINKS SHE HAS FRIENDS IN ATHEIA WHO CAN HELP US.

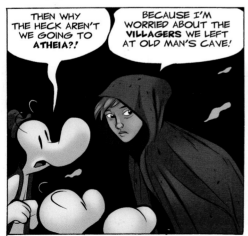

THEN WHY THE HECK AREN'T WE GOING TO **ATHEIA?!**

BECAUSE I'M WORRIED ABOUT THE **VILLAGERS** WE LEFT AT OLD MAN'S CAVE!

. . . AND I'M WORRIED ABOUT **LUCIUS** - -

CAN'T YOU PEOPLE TALK SOMEWHERE **ELSE?** I'M TRYING TO LISTEN FOR SIGNS OF LIFE!

LET'S ALL STEP OVER HERE FOR A MOMENT AND LET GRAN'MA LISTEN.

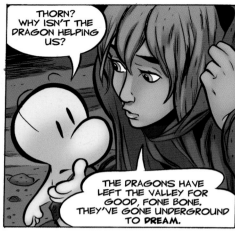

THORN? WHY ISN'T THE DRAGON HELPING US?

THE DRAGONS HAVE LEFT THE VALLEY FOR GOOD, FONE BONE. THEY'VE GONE UNDERGROUND TO **DREAM.**

WHAT?! THEY'RE GONNA **SLEEP** WHILE THE RAT CREATURES AND THE LORD OF THE LOCUSTS **DESTROY THEIR VALLEY?!**

IT'S NOT THEIR VALLEY ANYMORE. THEY FOUGHT THE LOCUST ONCE... NOW IT'S OUR TURN.

OUR TURN?! WHAT KIND OF A COP OUT IS **THAT?** I SAY WE WAKE 'EM **UP!**

GRAN'MA **TRIED** TO GET THE DRAGONS TO STAY, BUT THEY **WOULDN'T!**

YOU GUYS WORRY TOO MUCH ABOUT DRAGONS!

THEY **ABANDONED** YOU -- FORGET ABOUT 'EM!

YOU OUGHTA BE MORE SELF-SUFFICIENT, LIKE **ME!**

SST!

THORN!

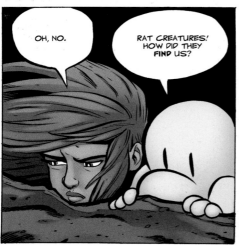

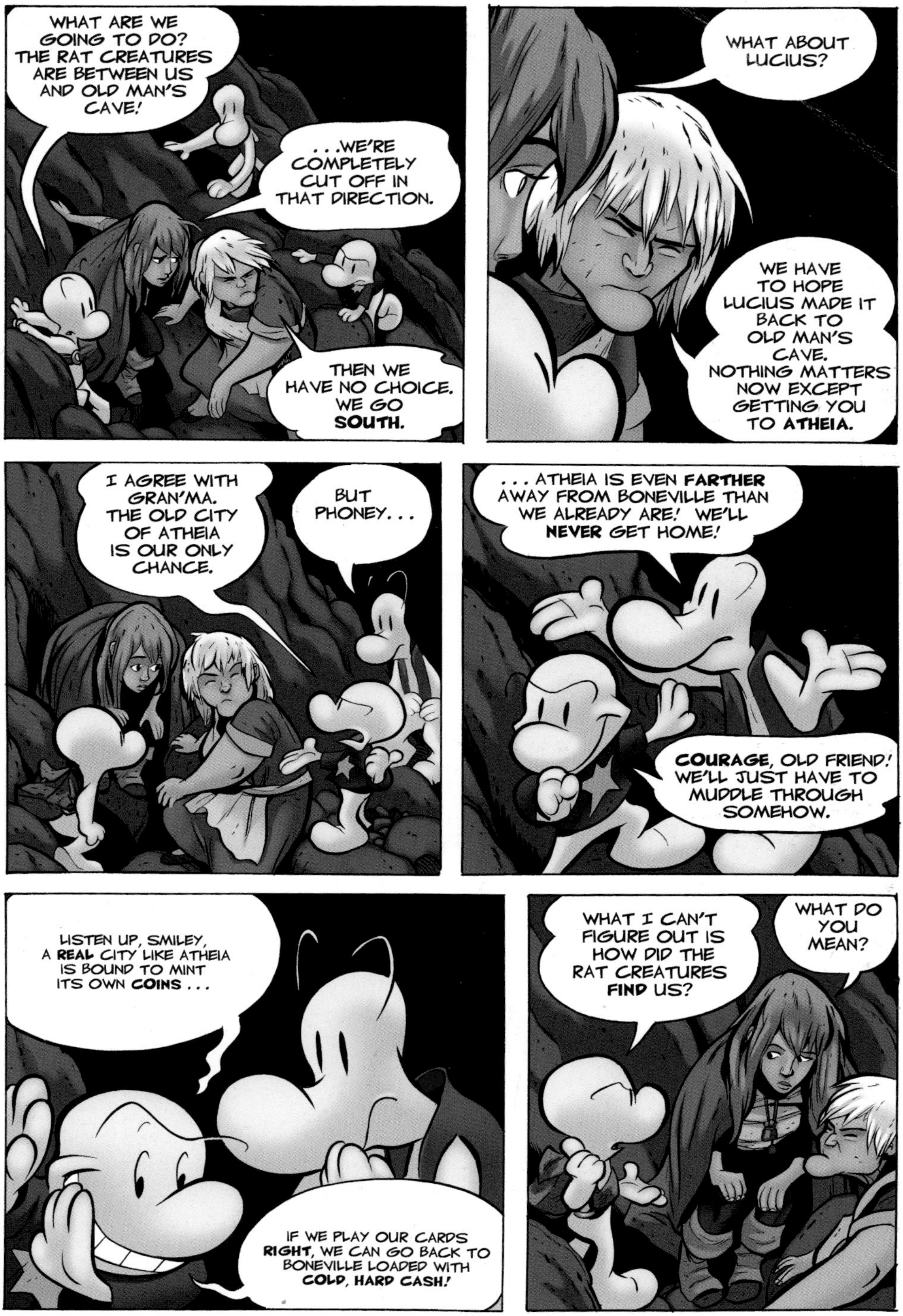
WHAT ARE WE GOING TO DO? THE RAT CREATURES ARE BETWEEN US AND OLD MAN'S CAVE!
. . .WE'RE COMPLETELY CUT OFF IN THAT DIRECTION.
THEN WE HAVE NO CHOICE. WE GO **SOUTH.**
WHAT ABOUT LUCIUS?
WE HAVE TO HOPE LUCIUS MADE IT BACK TO OLD MAN'S CAVE. NOTHING MATTERS NOW EXCEPT GETTING YOU TO **ATHEIA.**
I AGREE WITH GRAN'MA. THE OLD CITY OF ATHEIA IS OUR ONLY CHANCE.
BUT PHONEY. . .
. . . ATHEIA IS EVEN **FARTHER** AWAY FROM BONEVILLE THAN WE ALREADY ARE! WE'LL **NEVER** GET HOME!
COURAGE, OLD FRIEND! WE'LL JUST HAVE TO MUDDLE THROUGH SOMEHOW.
LISTEN UP, SMILEY, A **REAL** CITY LIKE ATHEIA IS BOUND TO MINT ITS OWN **COINS** . . .
IF WE PLAY OUR CARDS **RIGHT**, WE CAN GO BACK TO BONEVILLE LOADED WITH **COLD, HARD CASH!**
WHAT I CAN'T FIGURE OUT IS HOW DID THE RAT CREATURES **FIND** US?
WHAT DO YOU MEAN?

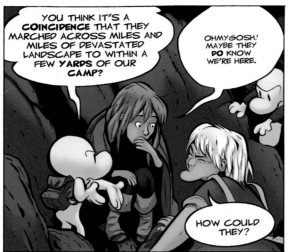

YOU THINK IT'S A **COINCIDENCE** THAT THEY MARCHED ACROSS MILES AND MILES OF DEVASTATED LANDSCAPE TO WITHIN A FEW **YARDS** OF OUR CAMP?

OHMYGOSH! MAYBE THEY **DO** KNOW WE'RE HERE.

HOW COULD THEY?

WHEN FONE BONE AND I DISTURBED THE **GHOST CIRCLE** -- THAT COULD'VE GIVEN US AWAY!

IMPOSSIBLE! WITHOUT **BRIAR**, THE RATS CAN'T SEE ANYTHING THAT HAPPENS IN THE DREAMING. AND BRIAR IS **DEAD**.

EVEN WITHOUT YOUR SISTER, **SOMETHING** GUIDED THOSE CREATURES HERE.

MAYBE THEY SAW OUR CAMPFIRE LAST NIGHT.

I THINK WE SHOULD GET OUT OF HERE.

I AGREE. LET'S GO.

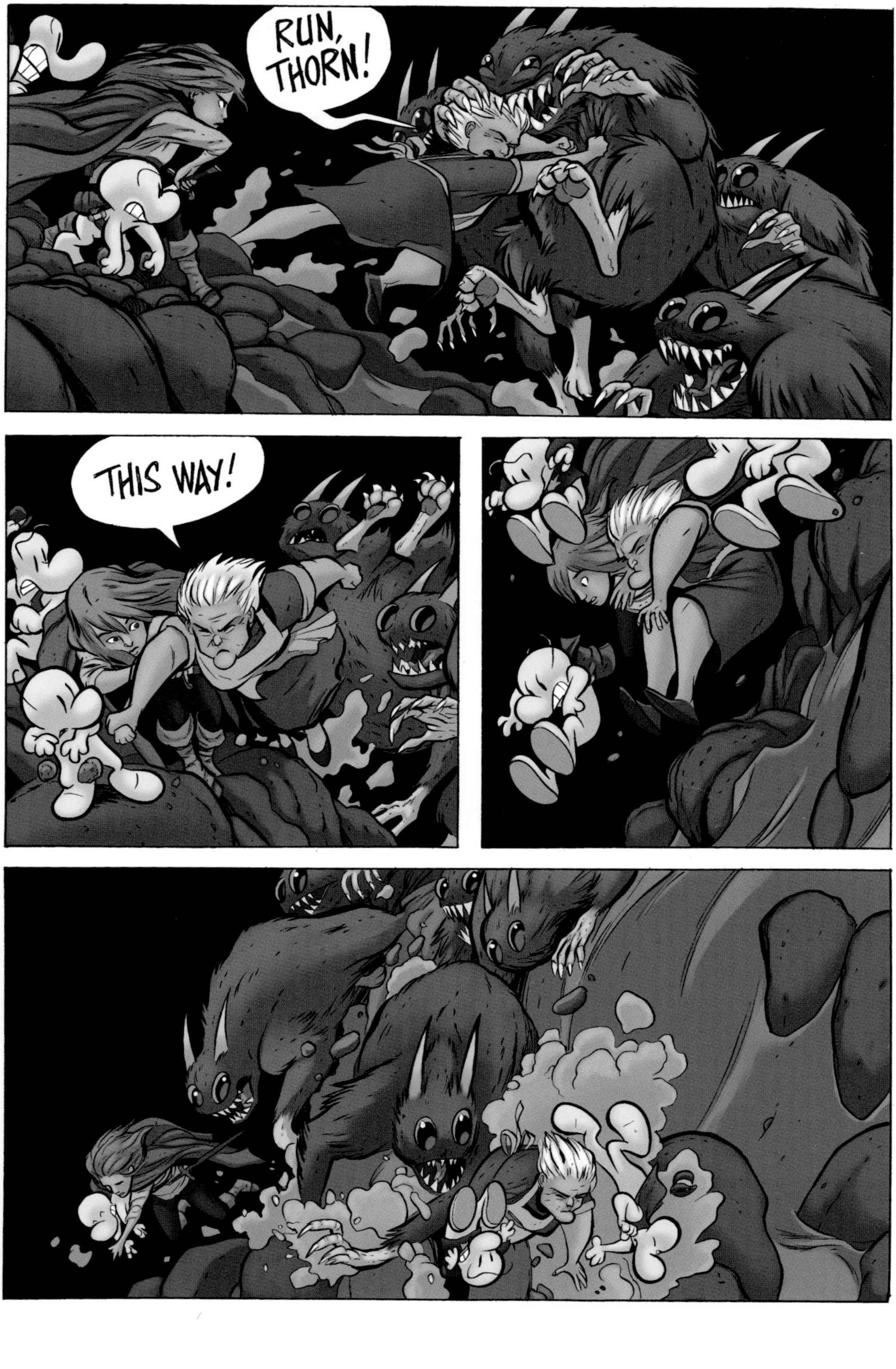
RUN, THORN!
THIS WAY!

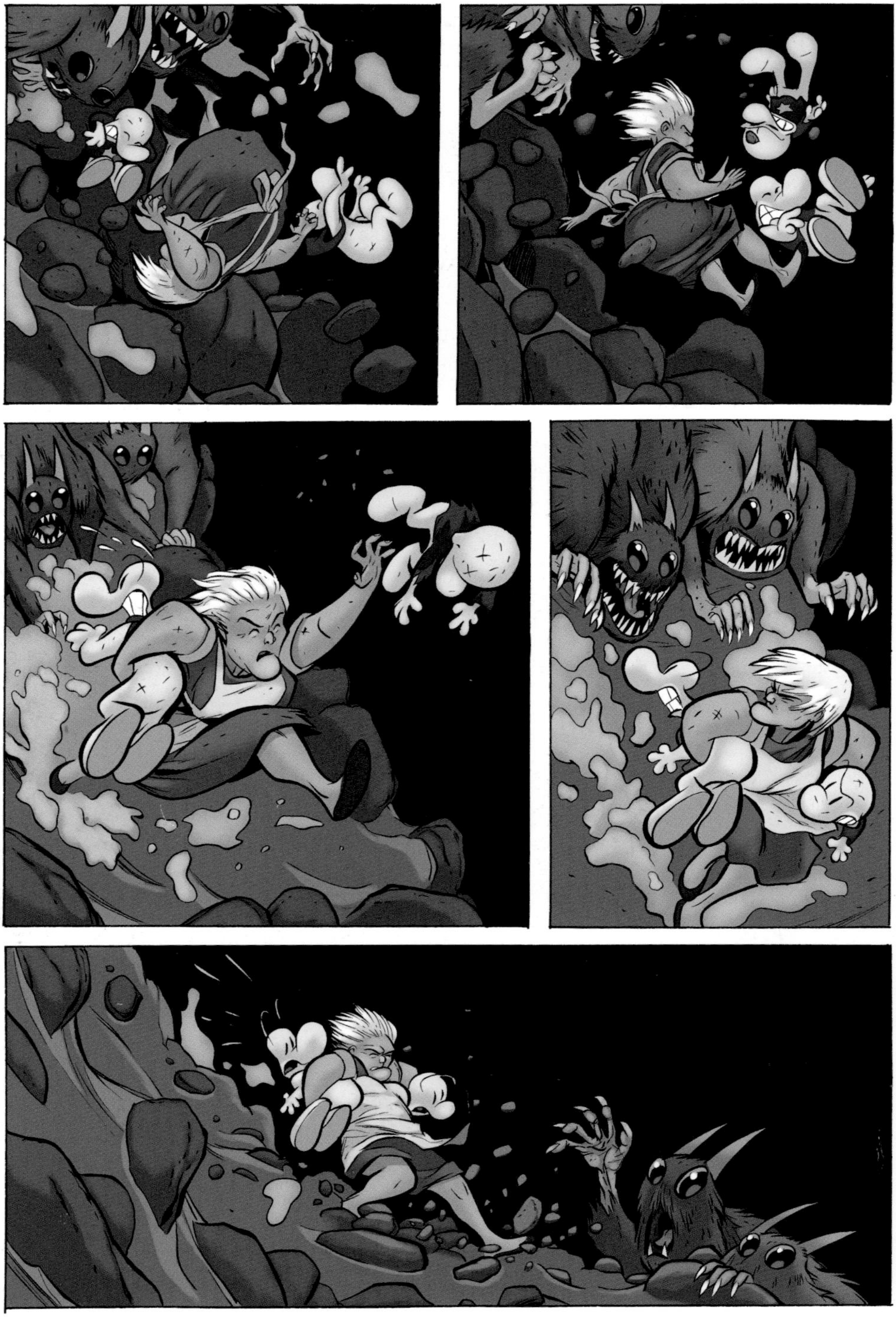

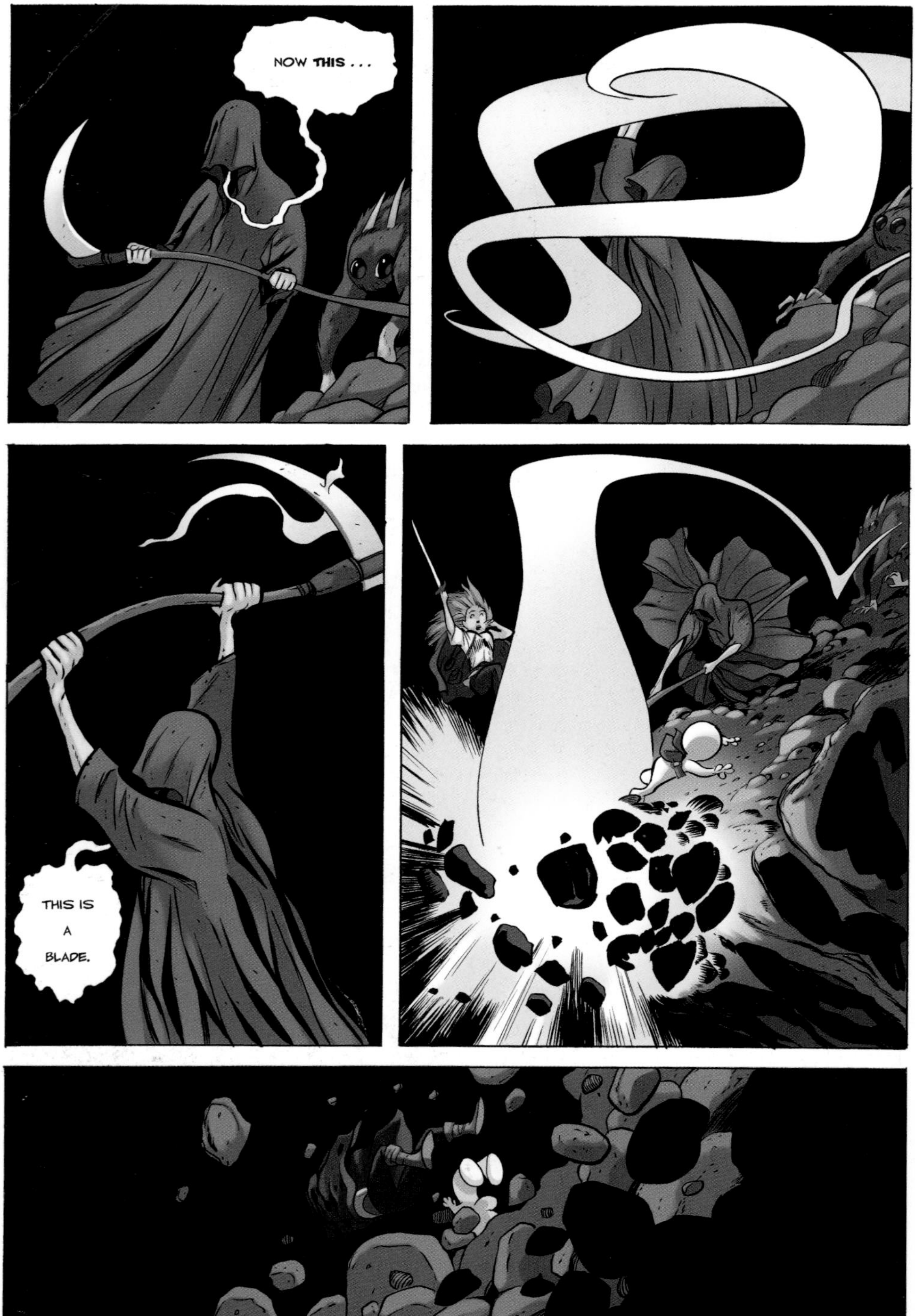
NOW THIS . . .
THIS IS A BLADE.

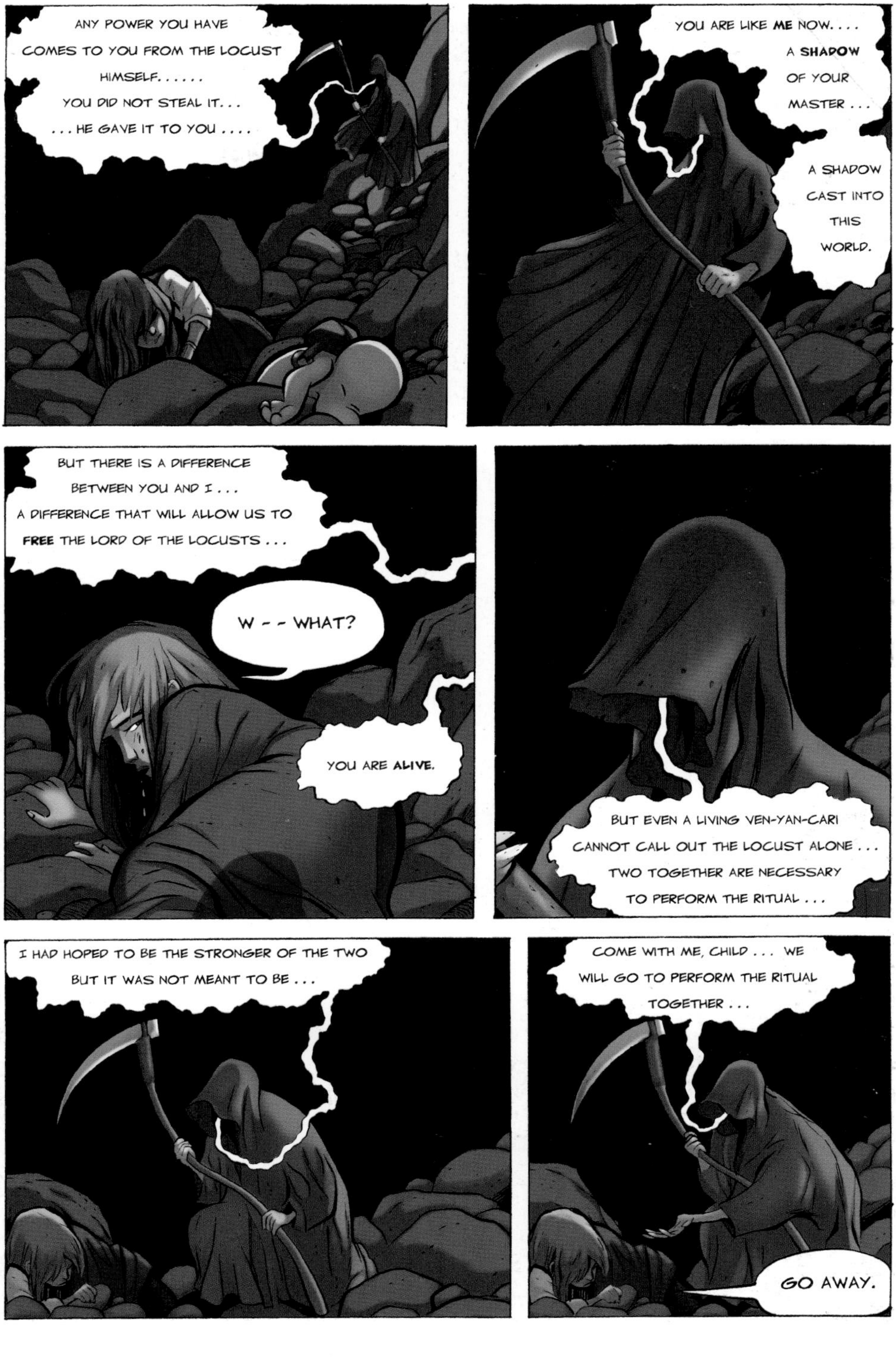
ANY POWER YOU HAVE COMES TO YOU FROM THE LOCUST HIMSELF...... YOU DID NOT STEAL IT... ...HE GAVE IT TO YOU....
YOU ARE LIKE ME NOW.... A SHADOW OF YOUR MASTER...
A SHADOW CAST INTO THIS WORLD.
BUT THERE IS A DIFFERENCE BETWEEN YOU AND I... A DIFFERENCE THAT WILL ALLOW US TO FREE THE LORD OF THE LOCUSTS...
W--WHAT?
YOU ARE ALIVE.
BUT EVEN A LIVING VEN-YAN-CARI CANNOT CALL OUT THE LOCUST ALONE... TWO TOGETHER ARE NECESSARY TO PERFORM THE RITUAL...
I HAD HOPED TO BE THE STRONGER OF THE TWO BUT IT WAS NOT MEANT TO BE...
COME WITH ME, CHILD... WE WILL GO TO PERFORM THE RITUAL TOGETHER...
GO AWAY.

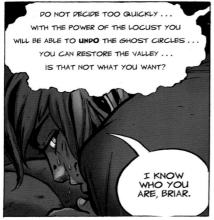

DO NOT DECIDE TOO QUICKLY . . . WITH THE POWER OF THE LOCUST YOU WILL BE ABLE TO **UNDO** THE GHOST CIRCLES . . . YOU CAN RESTORE THE VALLEY . . . IS THAT NOT WHAT YOU WANT?

I KNOW WHO YOU ARE, BRIAR.

I KNOW IT WAS YOU WHO TOLD THE RAT CREATURES WHERE TO FIND MY MOTHER AND FATHER SO YOU COULD **KILL** THEM!

IT WAS NOT I WHO KILLED YOUR PARENTS . . .

BUT **THEY** WHO KILLED **ME** . . . .

LIAR!

BUT IF I HAD, COULD YOU BLAME ME? YOUR ENTIRE FAMILY TREATED ME LIKE AN OLD NURSEMAID.

NO ONE KNEW **I** WAS A **VENI-YAN-CARI** LIKE YOU . . .

YES, **I** LED THEM TO THE RATS.

BUT WHEN YOUR MOTHER REALIZED I WAS KIDNAPPING YOU FOR THE **RITUAL** . . .

. . . YOUR FATHER CUT ME IN HALF WITH AN OLD ABANDONED FARM TOOL.

ONLY LATER DID I LEARN THAT YOUR PARENTS WERE **EATEN ALIVE** . . .

uhh...

THE WORLD IS FILLED WITH DARK TRUTHS, YOUNG ONE . . . AND ONE TRUTH I HAVE LEARNED IS DESTINY ALWAYS PREVAILS . . .

NOW **RISE** . . . TAKE MY HAND.

ON THE NEXT FULL MOON WE WILL PERFORM THE RITUAL . . .

YOU HAVE THE LOCUST INSIDE YOU NOW ... IT CONTROLS YOU ... IT WILL NOT ALLOW YOU TO RESIST ...

SPLAT!

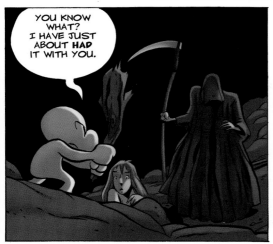

YOU KNOW WHAT? I HAVE JUST ABOUT **HAD** IT WITH YOU.

FIRST YOU MESSED WITH MY COUSIN, NOW YOU'RE MESSIN' WITH MY GIRL!

LET'S GO - -

RIGHT NOW!

THERE IS A PIECE OF THE LOCUST INSIDE OF **YOU** AS WELL ...

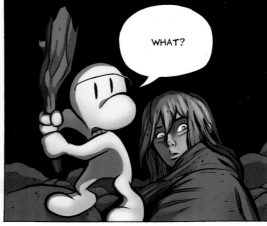

WHAT?

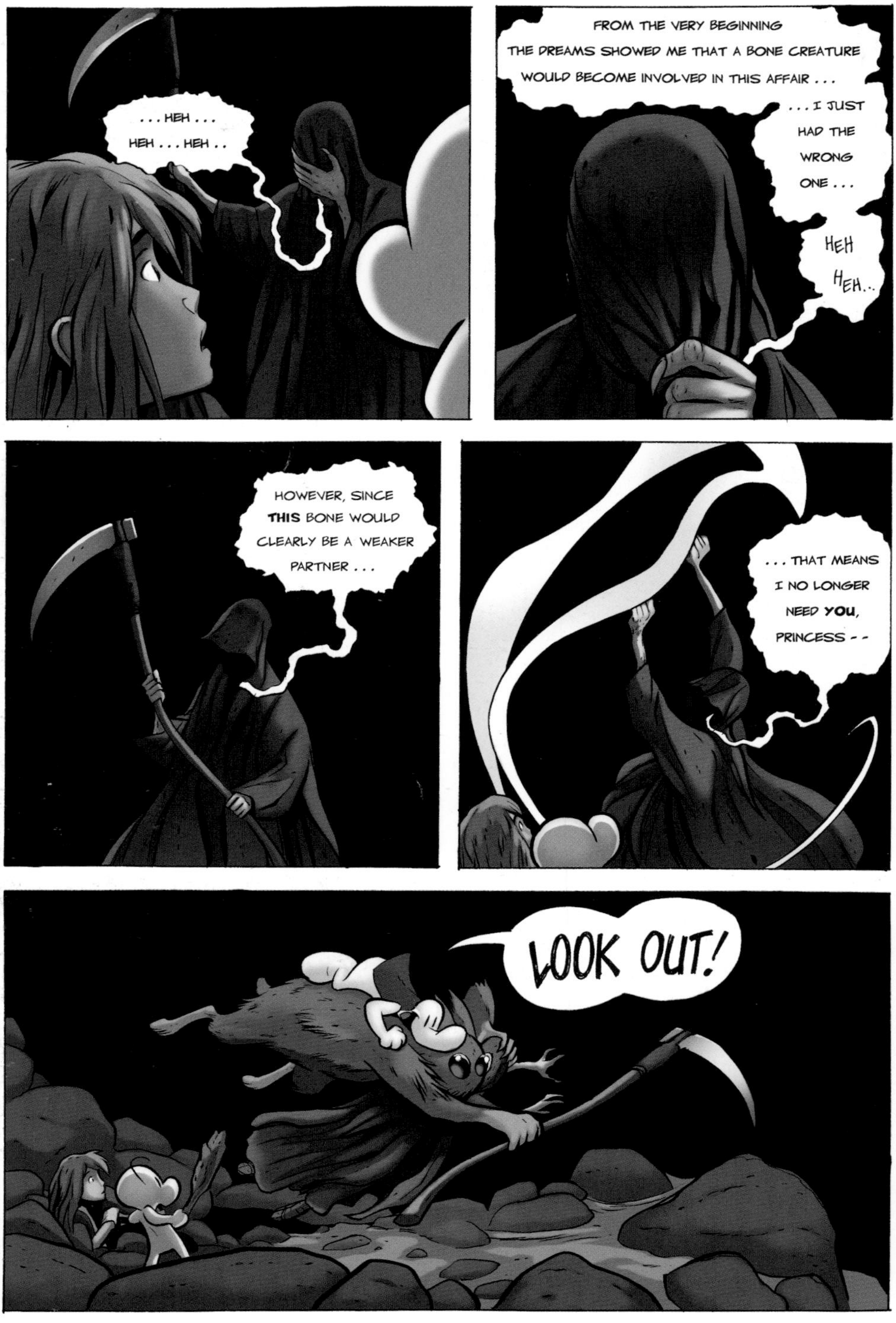
. . . HEH . . .
HEH . . . HEH . .
FROM THE VERY BEGINNING THE DREAMS SHOWED ME THAT A BONE CREATURE WOULD BECOME INVOLVED IN THIS AFFAIR . . .
. . . I JUST HAD THE WRONG ONE . . .
HEH HEH. . .
HOWEVER, SINCE **THIS** BONE WOULD CLEARLY BE A WEAKER PARTNER . . .
. . . THAT MEANS I NO LONGER NEED **YOU**, PRINCESS - -
LOOK OUT!

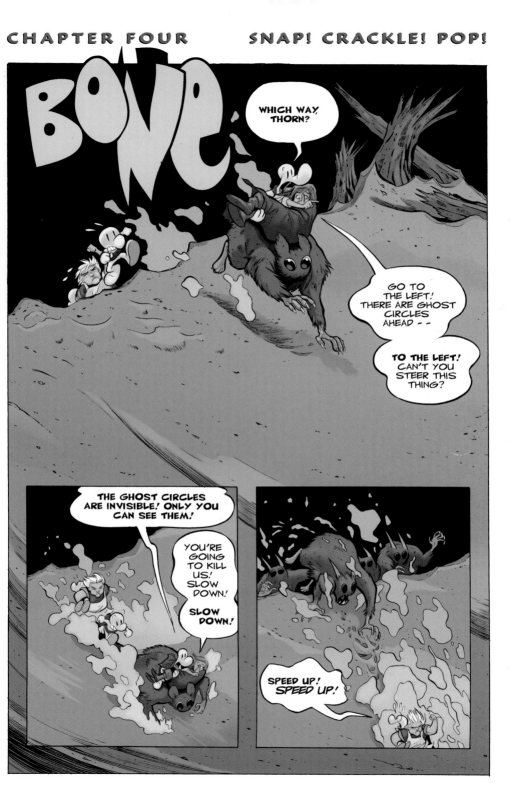

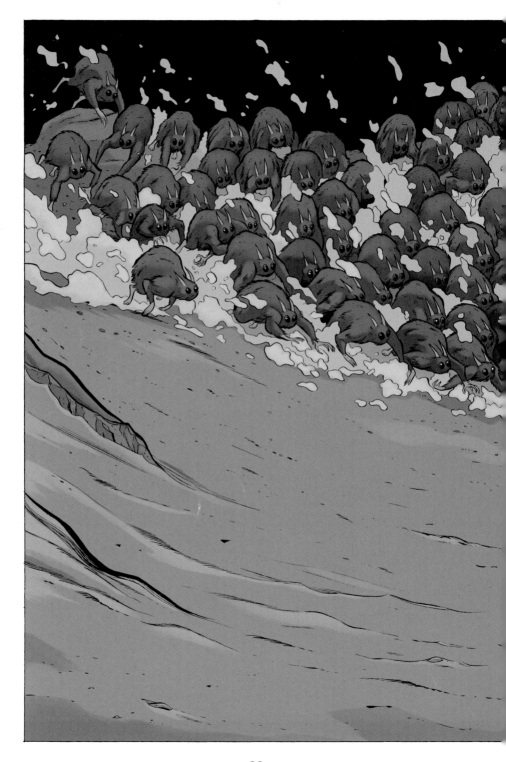

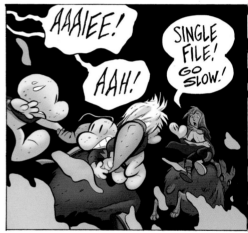

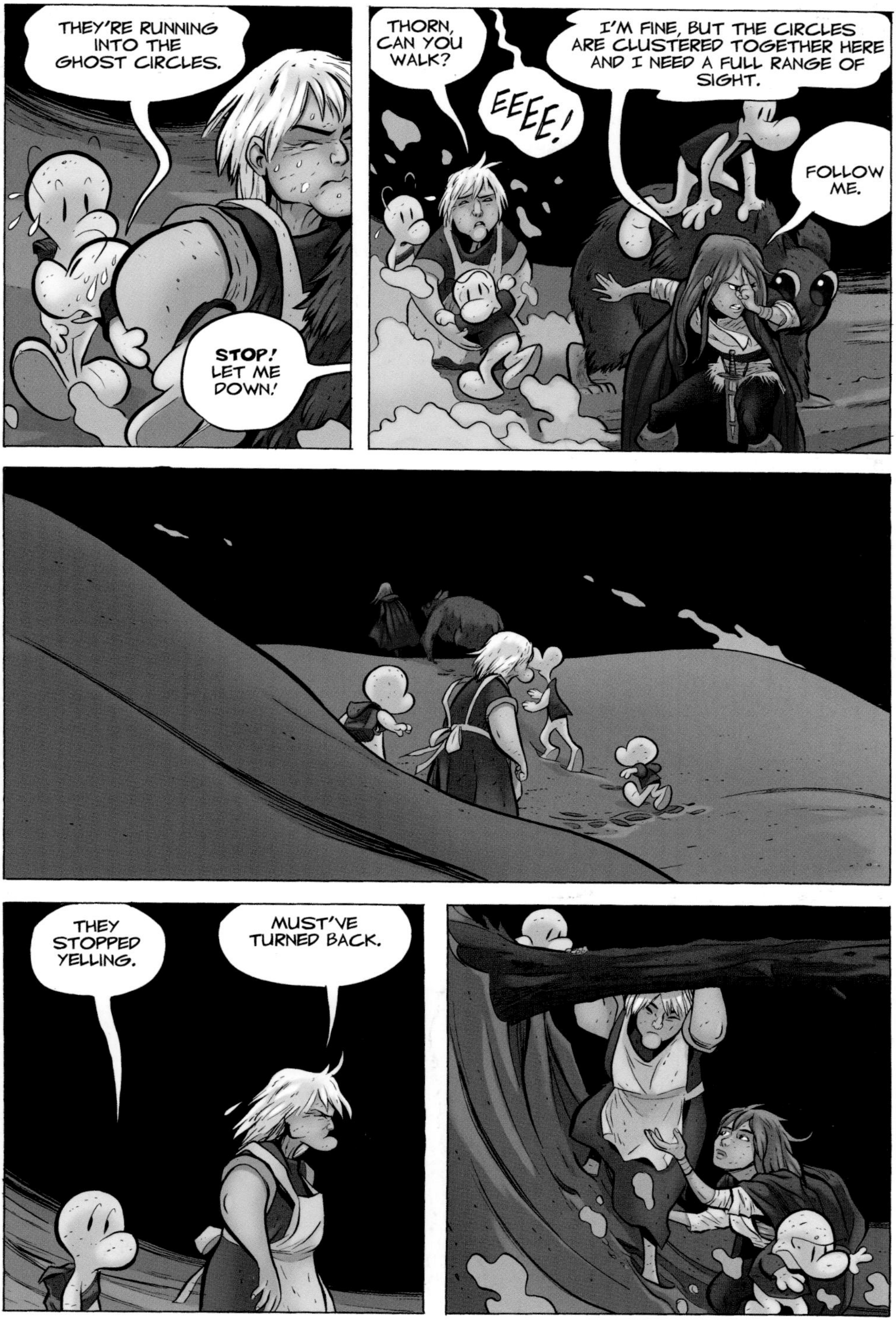
THEY'RE RUNNING INTO THE GHOST CIRCLES.
STOP! LET ME DOWN!
THORN, CAN YOU WALK?
EEEE!
I'M FINE, BUT THE CIRCLES ARE CLUSTERED TOGETHER HERE AND I NEED A FULL RANGE OF SIGHT.
FOLLOW ME.
THEY STOPPED YELLING.
MUST'VE TURNED BACK.

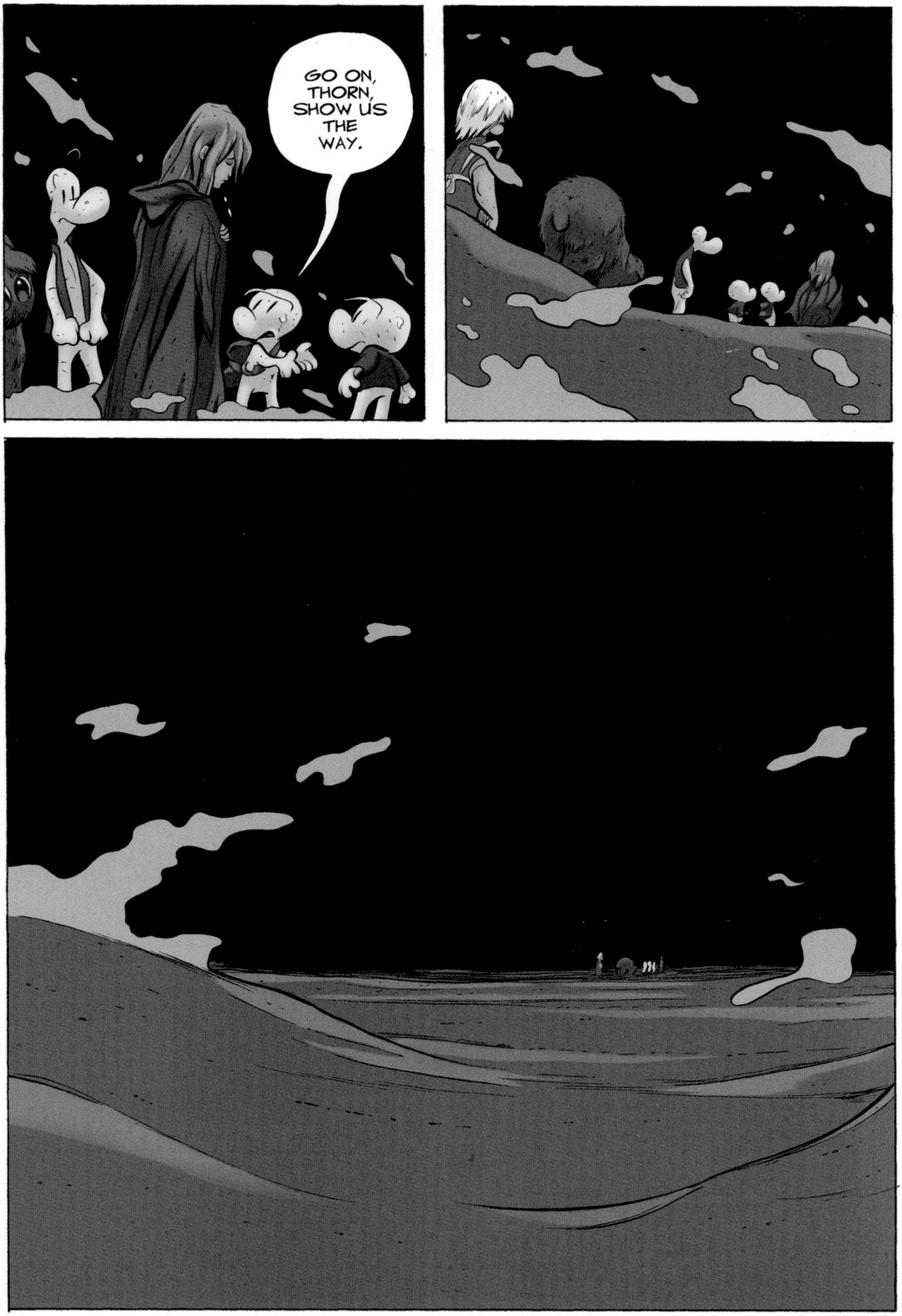
GO ON, THORN, SHOW US THE WAY.

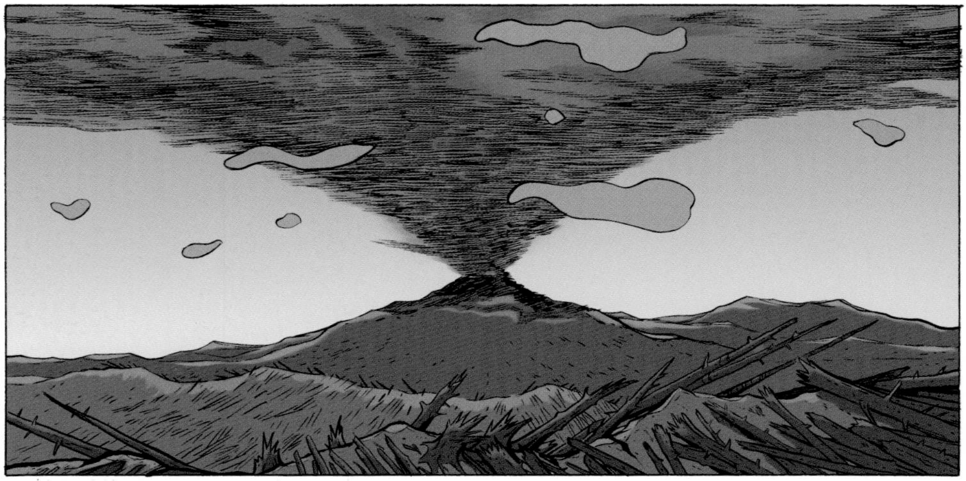

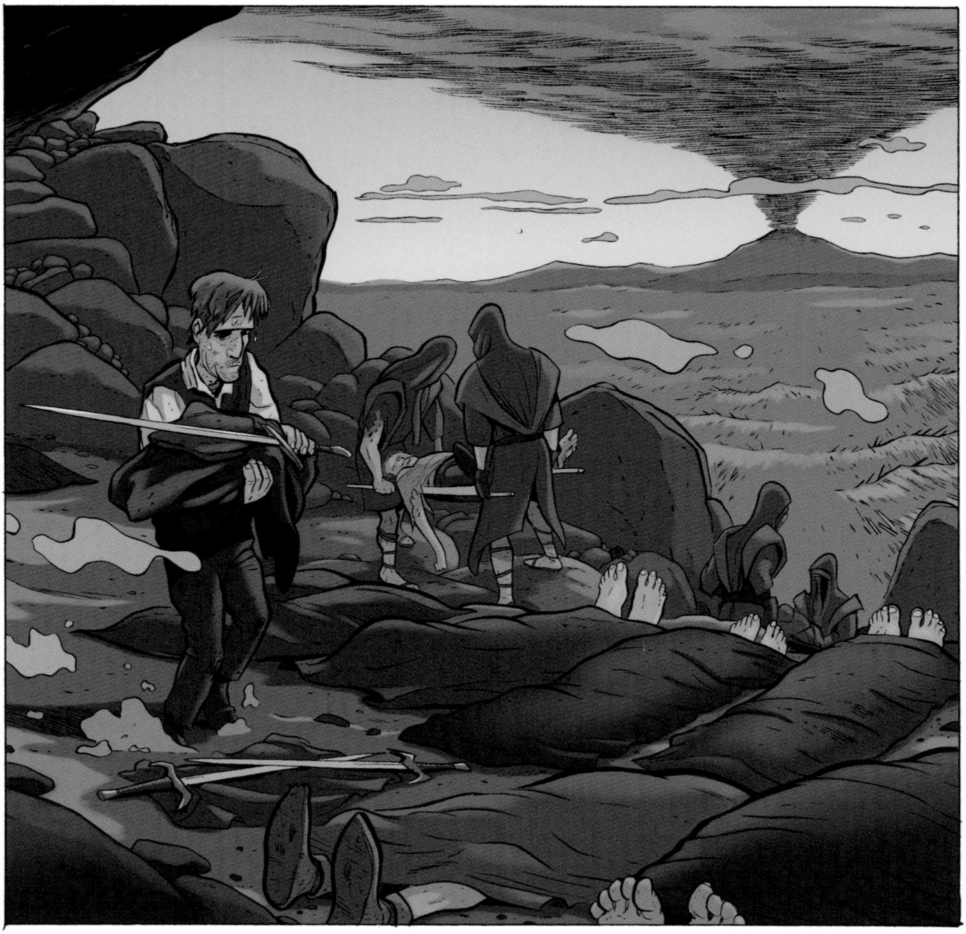

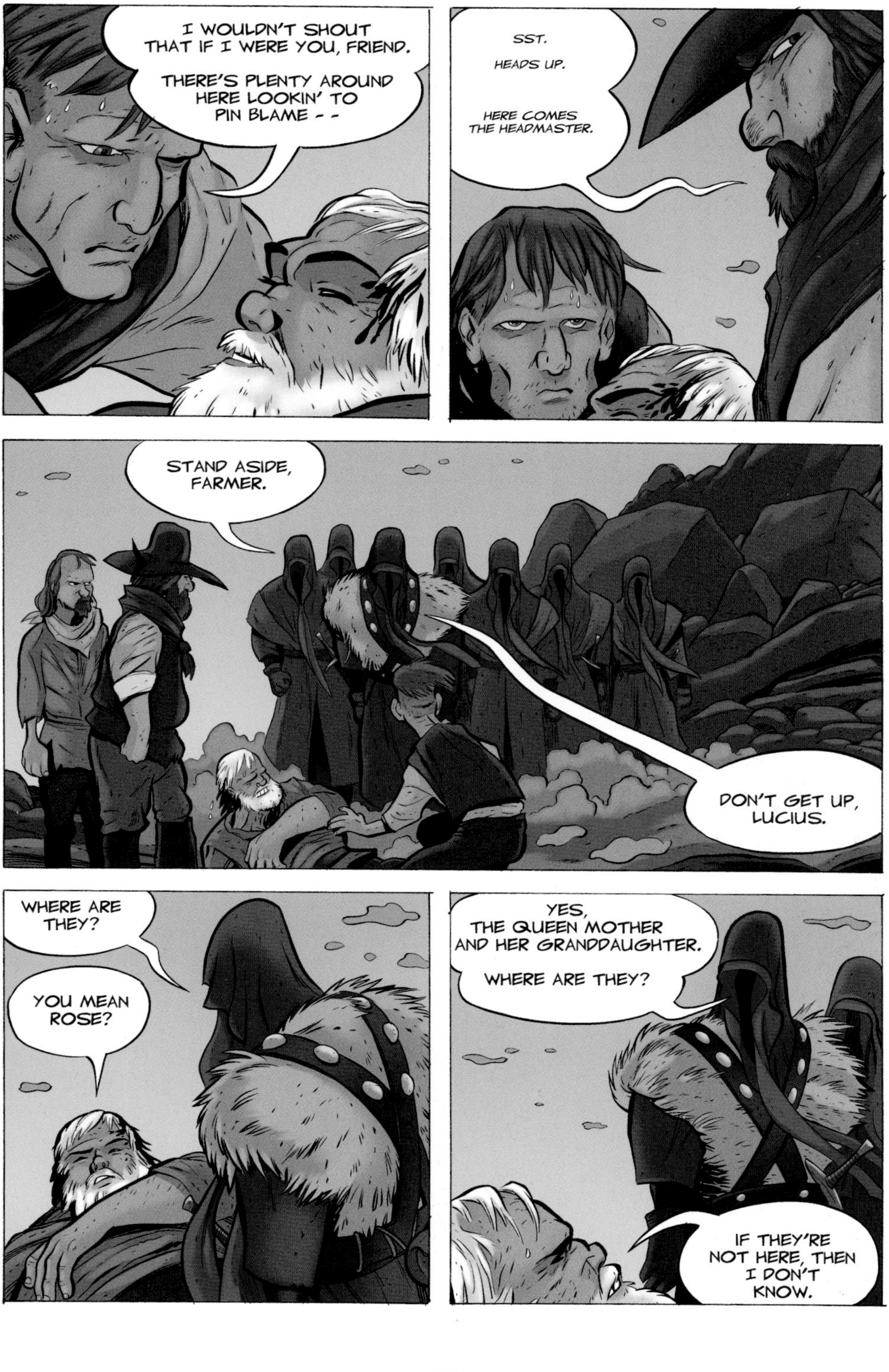
I WOULDN'T SHOUT THAT IF I WERE YOU, FRIEND.
THERE'S PLENTY AROUND HERE LOOKIN' TO PIN BLAME - -
SST.
HEADS UP.
HERE COMES THE HEADMASTER.
STAND ASIDE, FARMER.
DON'T GET UP, LUCIUS.
WHERE ARE THEY?
YOU MEAN ROSE?
YES, THE QUEEN MOTHER AND HER GRANDDAUGHTER.
WHERE ARE THEY?
IF THEY'RE NOT HERE, THEN I DON'T KNOW.

SHE WAS LAST SEEN WITH YOU AND A BONE CREATURE HEADING TOWARD THE MOUNTAIN...

...THE MOUNTAIN THAT HAS SINCE EXPLODED, FREEING THE LORD OF THE LOCUSTS.

I DON'T THINK YOU AND I WOULD BE ALIVE IF THE LOCUST WAS TRULY FREE.

AND IF **WE'RE** ALIVE, THEN MAYBE ROSE, THORN AND THE BONES ARE, TOO.

I KNOW IF ROSE SURVIVED, THEN SHE IS GOING SOUTH... TAKING THORN TO **ATHEIA.**

TO WHAT END? THE ANCIENT CAPITAL WENT DARK YEARS AGO. THERE IS NOTHING LEFT.

IT'S THE SEAT OF THE THRONE. SHE AND THORN ARE GOING TO REUNITE OUR PEOPLE AGAINST THE ENEMY.

WE SHOULD GO, TOO.

IMMEDIATELY.

NO.

THE ONLY SURVIVORS OF THIS DISASTER ARE THE MEMBERS OF OUR ORDER AND YOUR VILLAGERS WHO WERE IN THE CAVE WITH US.

THE WAR IS OVER AND WE LOST.

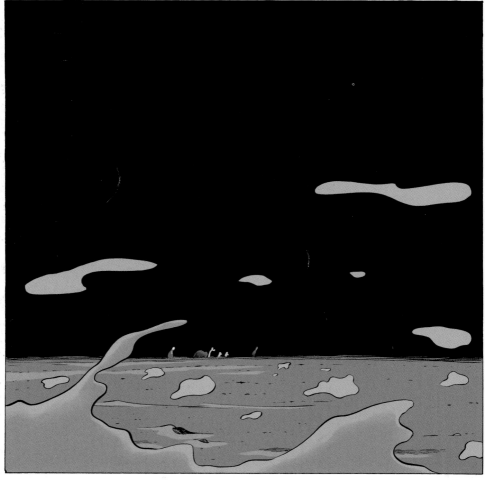

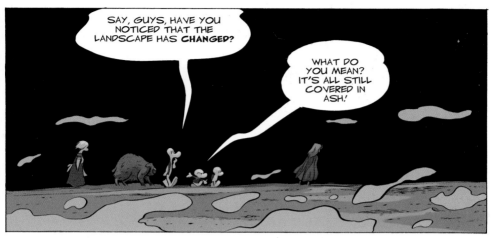

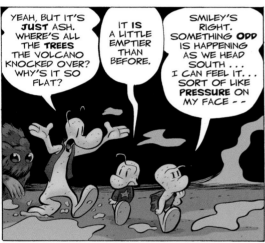

IT'S STRANGE, GRAN'MA. . . THE GHOST CIRCLES SHOULD BE THINNING OUT AS WE GET FARTHER FROM THE MOUNTAIN, BUT INSTEAD THEY SEEM TO BE GROWING **HEAVIER** UP AHEAD.

IT'S ALMOST AS IF WE'VE MET A **NEW** SYSTEM OF GHOST CIRCLES MOVING UP FROM THE SOUTH TOWARDS US.

BLOODY STARS.

YET OFF TO THE **EAST** TOWARD **PAWA**, THERE'S A NARROW REGION FREE FROM ANY GHOST CIRCLES WHATSOEVER.

HMM.

OKAY, **BREAK TIME.**

WE AIN'T GOIN' ANYWHERE FAST.

GHOST CIRCLES

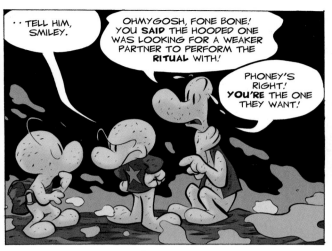

··TELL HIM, SMILEY.

OHMYGOSH, FONE BONE! YOU **SAID** THE HOODED ONE WAS LOOKING FOR A WEAKER PARTNER TO PERFORM THE **RITUAL** WITH.'

PHONEY'S RIGHT.' **YOU'RE** THE ONE THEY WANT.'

EVERYONE COME HERE.

WE'VE PLOTTED OUT A PATH.

WE CAN'T GO STRAIGHT THROUGH TO ATHEIA BECAUSE OF THE GHOST CIRCLES, BUT THORN HAS FOUND A PATH TO THE EAST.

IT'S A LONGER WAY AROUND, BUT IT'LL GET US THERE.

YOU SURE WE CAN TRUST YOUR COMPANION, HERE, SMILEY?

GEE, GRAN'MA! HE JUST SAVED OUR LIVES.'

ALL THE SAME, I'LL KEEP HIM IN FRONT OF ME WHERE I CAN SEE HIM.

CHEER UP, EVERYBODY, WE'RE ON OUR WAY NOW AND **NOTHIN'** CAN STOP US.'

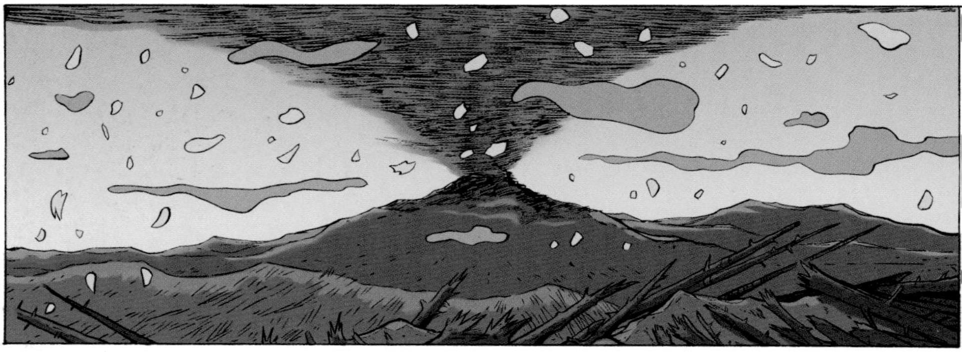

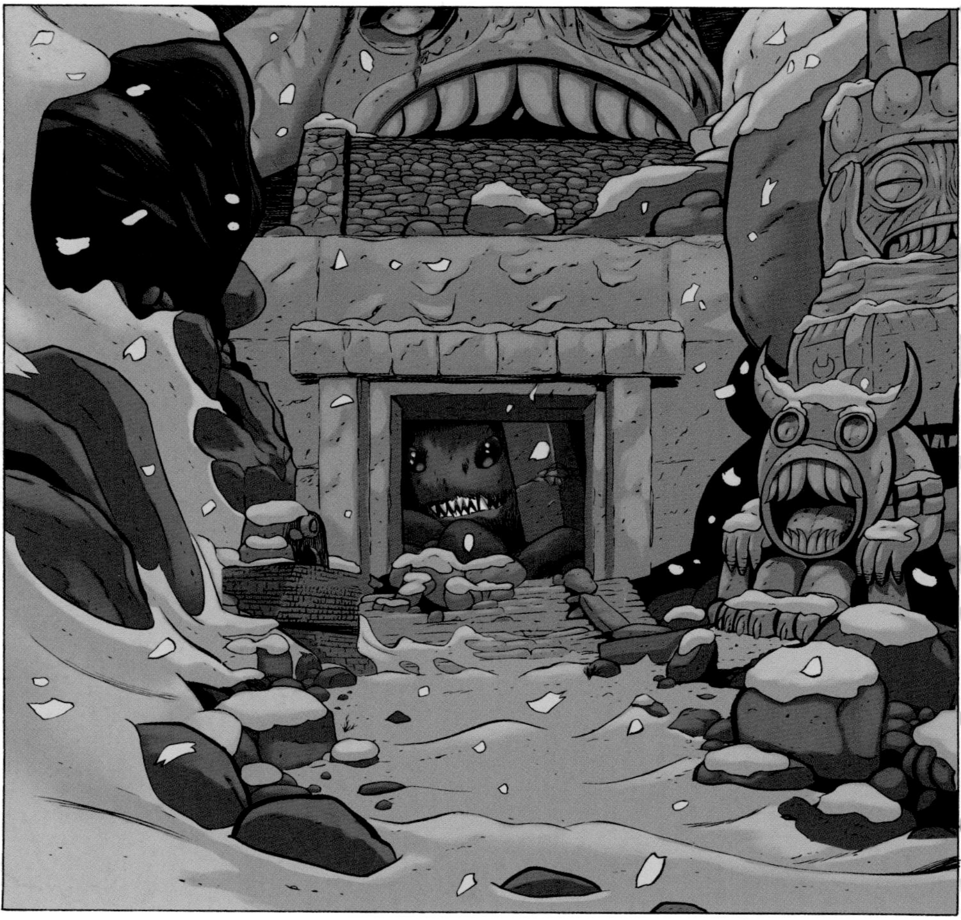

WHAT HAPPENED?

WHAT HAVE YOU DONE TO MY COUSIN?

HE COLLAPSED FROM HUNGER. JUST LIKE WE'RE **ALL** GOING TO IF WE DON'T FIND SOME FOOD SOON.

THORN! GET US SOMETHING -- **QUICK**, BEFORE SMILEY GETS WORSE!

ME? WHAT CAN I DO?

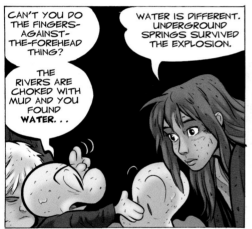

CAN'T YOU DO THE FINGERS-AGAINST-THE-FOREHEAD THING?

THE RIVERS ARE CHOKED WITH MUD AND YOU FOUND **WATER**. . .

WATER IS DIFFERENT. UNDERGROUND SPRINGS SURVIVED THE EXPLOSION.

ISN'T THERE SOME UNDERGROUND **FOOD**?

I'M SORRY, PHONEY. ANYTHING THAT WASN'T TRAPPED INSIDE A GHOST CIRCLE WAS DESTROYED.

THEN GO INSIDE A GHOST CIRCLE! THIS IS AN EMERGENCY!

SAY, WAIT A MINUTE. . .

YOU WANT ME TO GO INSIDE A GHOST CIRCLE?

NOT BY YOURSELF, BUT IF WE HELD HANDS LIKE BEFORE, MAYBE WE COULD GO INSIDE AND LOOK FOR A **FARM** OR A **GARDEN** . . .

I SUPPOSE WE **COULD**. . .

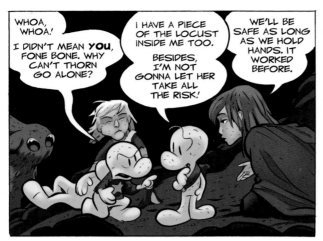

WHOA, WHOA!

I DIDN'T MEAN **YOU**, FONE BONE. WHY CAN'T THORN GO ALONE?

I HAVE A PIECE OF THE LOCUST INSIDE ME TOO.

BESIDES, I'M NOT GONNA LET HER TAKE ALL THE RISK!

WE'LL BE SAFE AS LONG AS WE HOLD HANDS. IT WORKED BEFORE.

IT WAS AN **ACCIDENT** BEFORE! HE'S NOT BUILT FOR DANGER THE WAY YOU ARE.

HEY!

GRAN'MA, WHERE ALONG THE RIVER ARE WE?

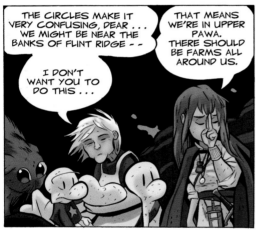

THE CIRCLES MAKE IT VERY CONFUSING, DEAR . . . WE MIGHT BE NEAR THE BANKS OF FLINT RIDGE - -

I DON'T WANT YOU TO DO THIS . . .

THAT MEANS WE'RE IN UPPER PAWA. THERE SHOULD BE FARMS ALL AROUND US.

GHOST CIRCLES ARE PART OF THE LOCUST HIMSELF. POISONOUS NIGHTMARES SENT FORTH TO DEMORALIZE AND CONTROL US.

LAST TIME YOU DID THIS, IT GAVE AWAY OUR POSITION TO THE ENEMY.

WE HAVE TO EAT.

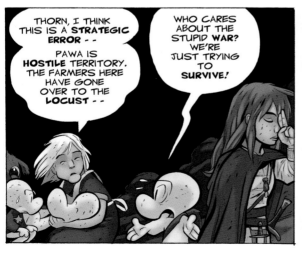

THORN, I THINK THIS IS A **STRATEGIC ERROR** - -

PAWA IS **HOSTILE** TERRITORY. THE FARMERS HERE HAVE GONE OVER TO THE **LOCUST** - -

WHO CARES ABOUT THE STUPID **WAR**? WE'RE JUST TRYING TO **SURVIVE!**

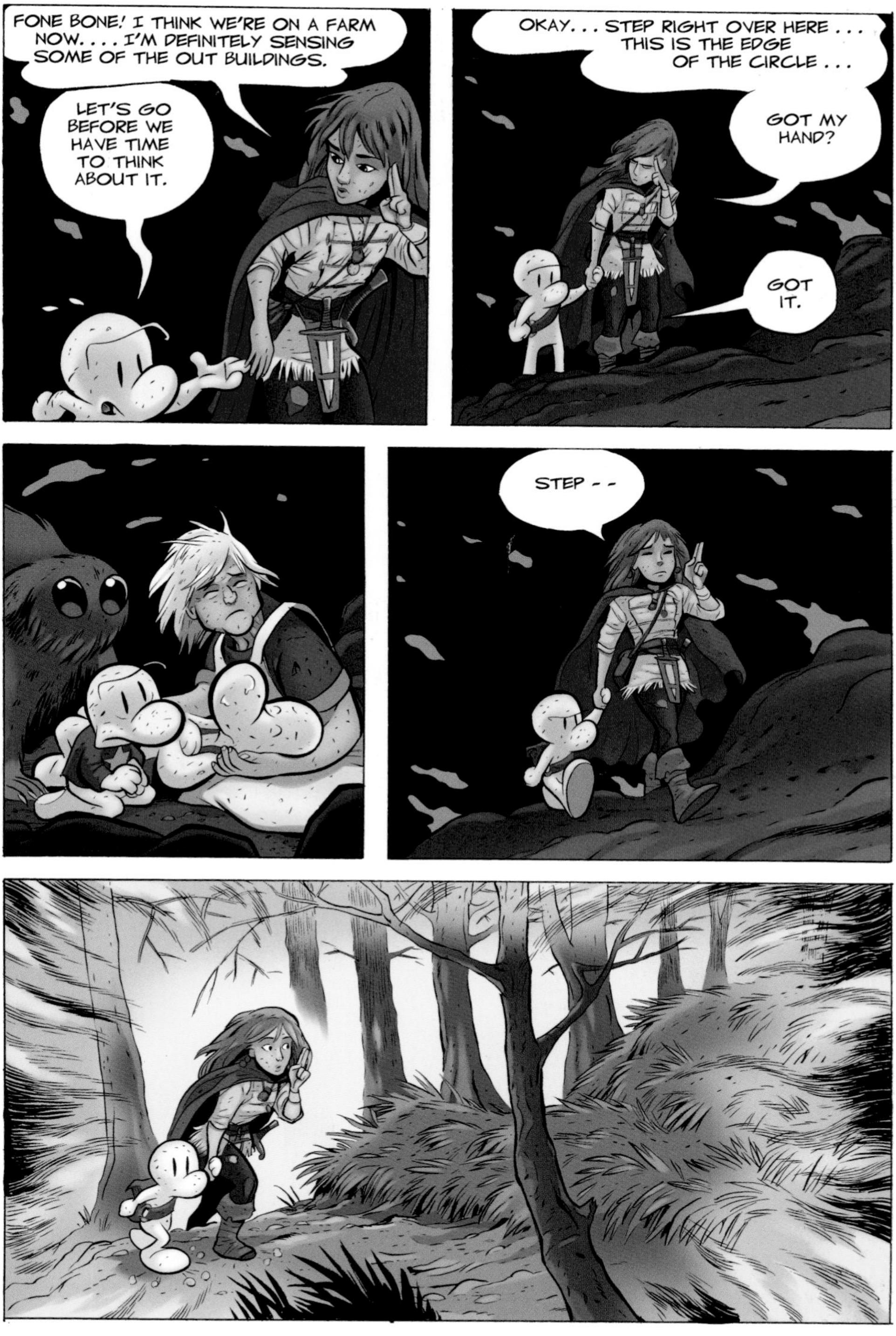
FONE BONE! I THINK WE'RE ON A FARM NOW. . . . I'M DEFINITELY SENSING SOME OF THE OUT BUILDINGS.
LET'S GO BEFORE WE HAVE TIME TO THINK ABOUT IT.
OKAY. . . STEP RIGHT OVER HERE . . . THIS IS THE EDGE OF THE CIRCLE . . .
GOT MY HAND?
GOT IT.
STEP - -

WE DID IT.

LOOK.

A ROOT CELLAR!

THERE'S A FARMHOUSE UP ABOVE . . . IS ANYONE HOME?

I THINK SO. YES . . . THERE'S A FAMILY INSIDE . . .

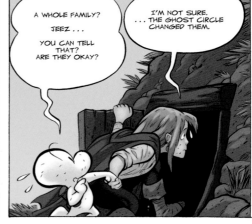

A WHOLE FAMILY? JEEZ . . . YOU CAN TELL THAT? ARE THEY OKAY?

I'M NOT SURE. . . . THE GHOST CIRCLE CHANGED THEM.

CHANGED THEM?!

WHAT'S **THAT** SUPPOSED TO MEAN?

THEY'RE DEFINIITELY NOT ALIVE . . .

. . . BUT THEY'RE MOVING AROUND.

C'MON. OPEN YOUR BACK- PACK.

MOVING AROUND?!

HOW? ARE THEY **ZOMBIES** OR SOMETHING?!

FONE BONE! HOLD TIGHT TO MY HAND! WE'RE INSIDE A **GHOST CIRCLE!**

I DON'T KNOW WHAT WILL HAPPEN IF WE LOSE CONTACT!

LET'S GET THESE APPLES AND GET OUT OF HERE!

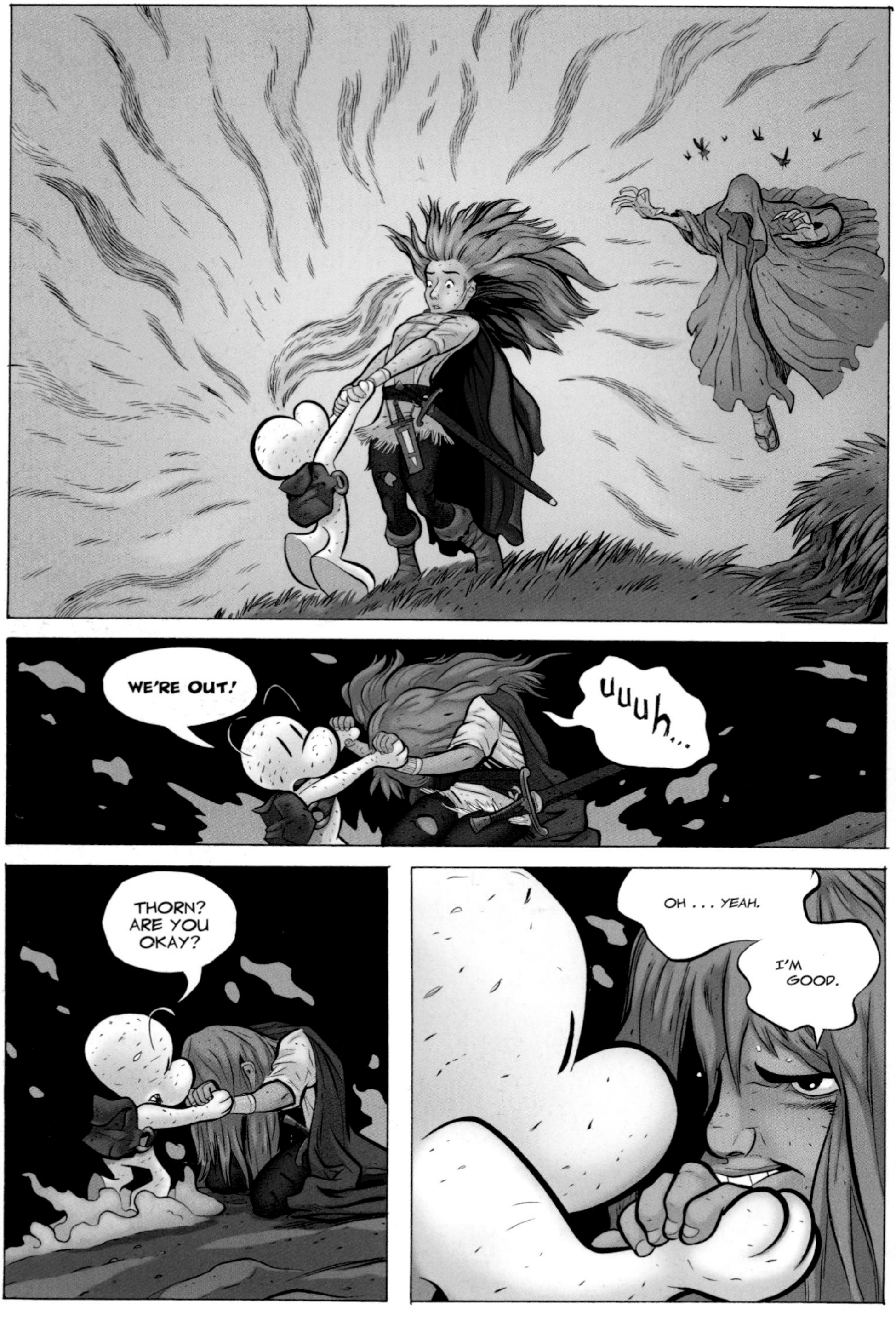
WE'RE OUT!
uuuh...
THORN? ARE YOU OKAY?
OH . . . YEAH.
I'M GOOD.

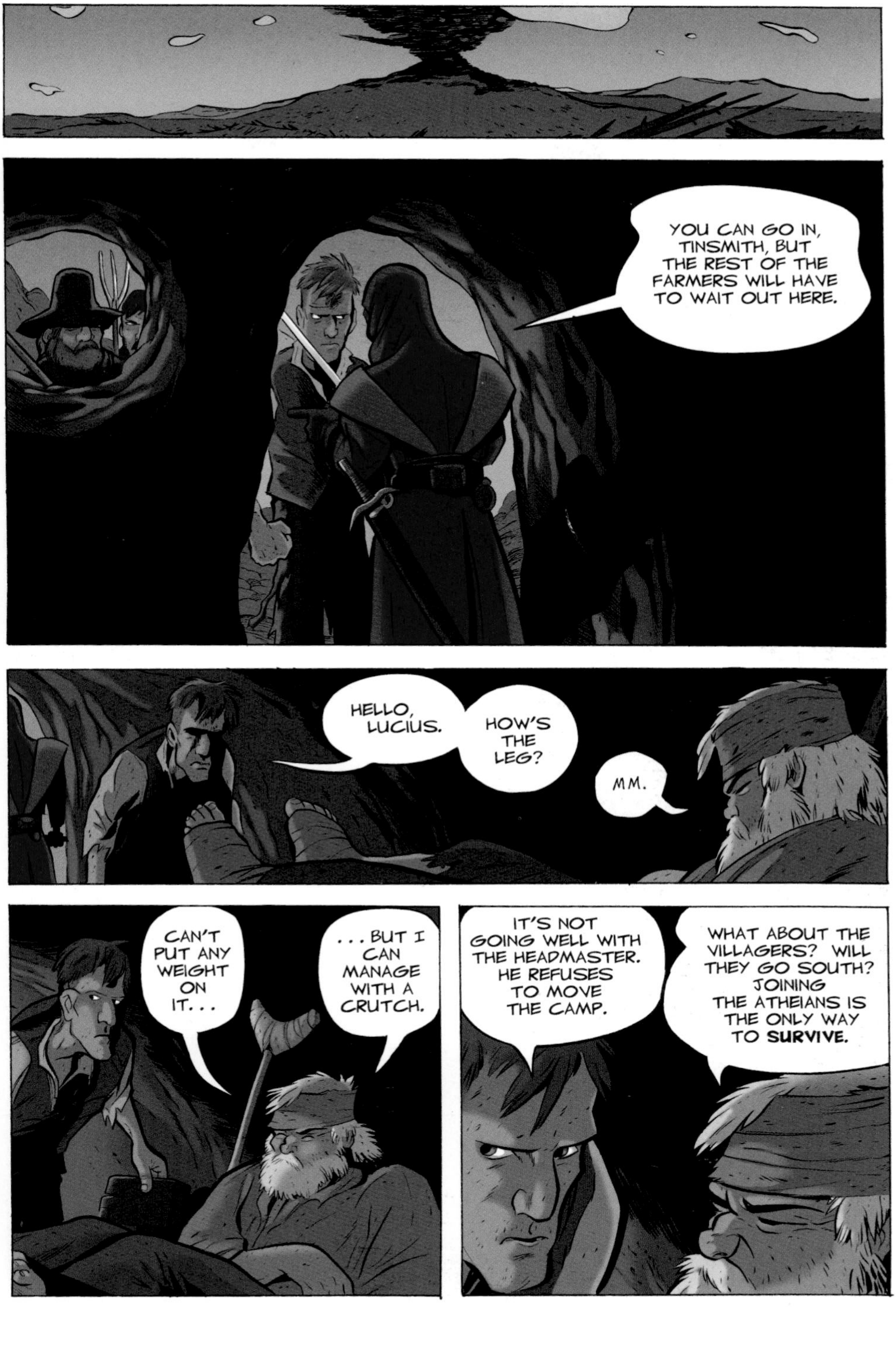
YOU CAN GO IN, TINSMITH, BUT THE REST OF THE FARMERS WILL HAVE TO WAIT OUT HERE.
HELLO, LUCIUS.
HOW'S THE LEG?
MM.
CAN'T PUT ANY WEIGHT ON IT...
...BUT I CAN MANAGE WITH A CRUTCH.
IT'S NOT GOING WELL WITH THE HEADMASTER. HE REFUSES TO MOVE THE CAMP.
WHAT ABOUT THE VILLAGERS? WILL THEY GO SOUTH? JOINING THE ATHEIANS IS THE ONLY WAY TO **SURVIVE.**

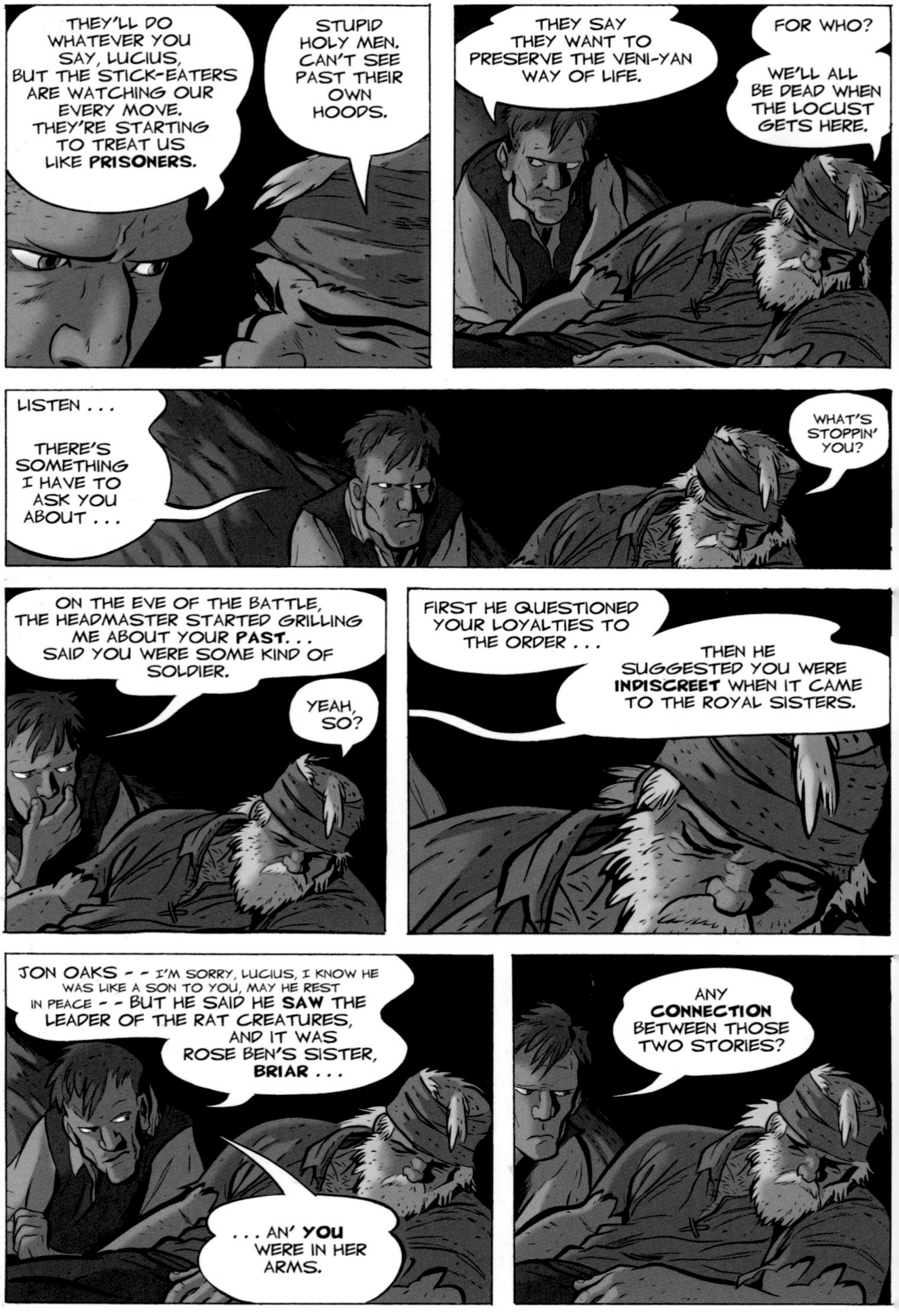
THEY'LL DO WHATEVER YOU SAY, LUCIUS, BUT THE STICK-EATERS ARE WATCHING OUR EVERY MOVE. THEY'RE STARTING TO TREAT US LIKE **PRISONERS.**
STUPID HOLY MEN. CAN'T SEE PAST THEIR OWN HOODS.
THEY SAY THEY WANT TO PRESERVE THE VENI-YAN WAY OF LIFE.
FOR WHO?
WE'LL ALL BE DEAD WHEN THE LOCUST GETS HERE.
LISTEN . . .
THERE'S SOMETHING I HAVE TO ASK YOU ABOUT . . .
WHAT'S STOPPIN' YOU?
ON THE EVE OF THE BATTLE, THE HEADMASTER STARTED GRILLING ME ABOUT YOUR **PAST** . . . SAID YOU WERE SOME KIND OF SOLDIER.
YEAH, SO?
FIRST HE QUESTIONED YOUR LOYALTIES TO THE ORDER . . .
THEN HE SUGGESTED YOU WERE **INDISCREET** WHEN IT CAME TO THE ROYAL SISTERS.
JON OAKS - - I'M SORRY, LUCIUS, I KNOW HE WAS LIKE A SON TO YOU, MAY HE REST IN PEACE - - BUT HE SAID HE **SAW** THE LEADER OF THE RAT CREATURES, AND IT WAS ROSE BEN'S SISTER, **BRIAR** . . .
. . . AN' **YOU** WERE IN HER ARMS.
ANY **CONNECTION** BETWEEN THOSE TWO STORIES?

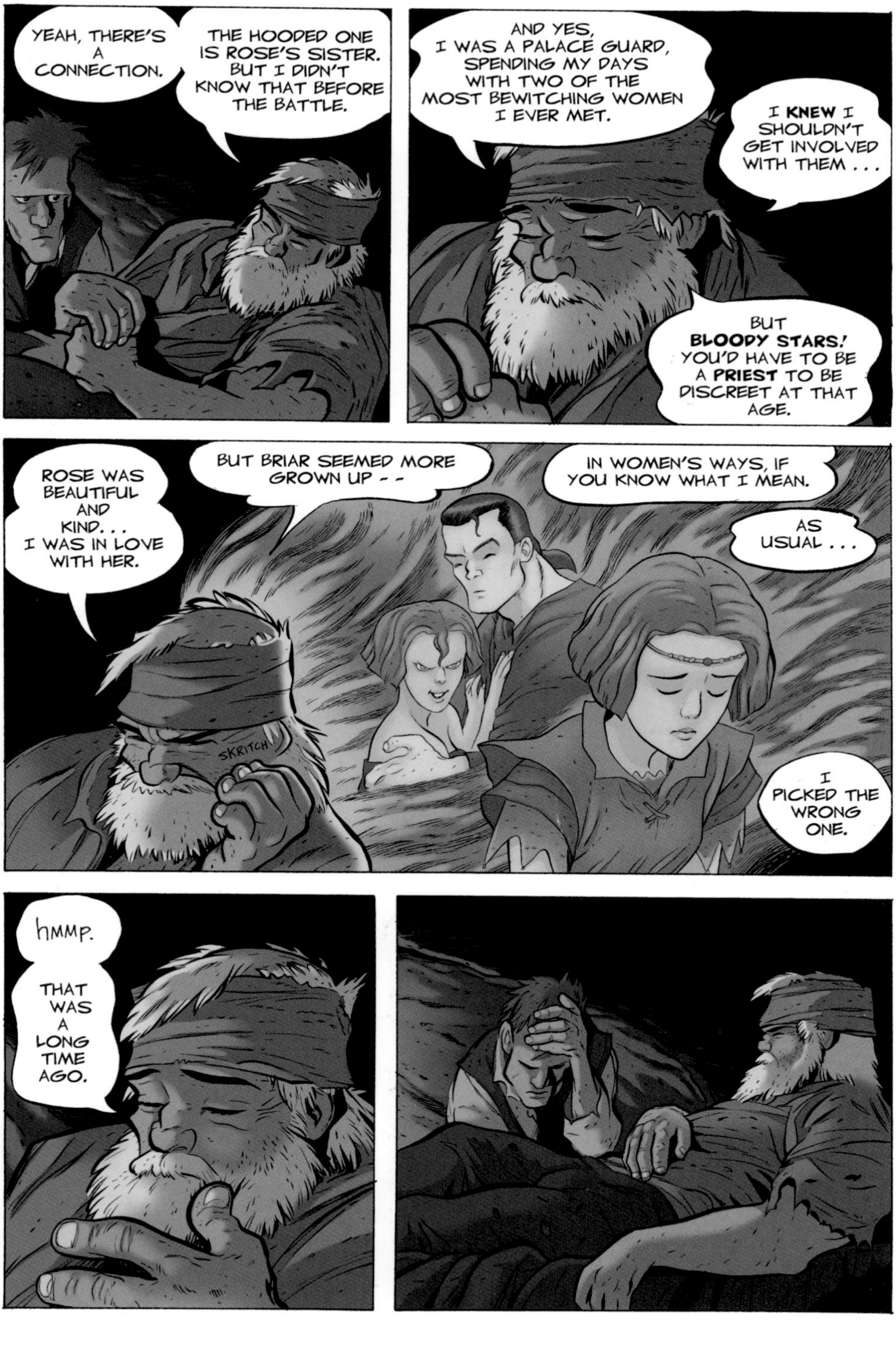
YEAH, THERE'S A CONNECTION.
THE HOODED ONE IS ROSE'S SISTER. BUT I DIDN'T KNOW THAT BEFORE THE BATTLE.
AND YES, I WAS A PALACE GUARD, SPENDING MY DAYS WITH TWO OF THE MOST BEWITCHING WOMEN I EVER MET.
I **KNEW** I SHOULDN'T GET INVOLVED WITH THEM . . .
BUT **BLOODY STARS!** YOU'D HAVE TO BE A **PRIEST** TO BE DISCREET AT THAT AGE.
ROSE WAS BEAUTIFUL AND KIND. . . I WAS IN LOVE WITH HER.
BUT BRIAR SEEMED MORE GROWN UP - -
IN WOMEN'S WAYS, IF YOU KNOW WHAT I MEAN.
AS USUAL . . .
SKRITCH
I PICKED THE WRONG ONE.
hmmp.
THAT WAS A LONG TIME AGO.

CRUNCH MUNCH!

NOBODY LIKED ME. THEY SAID I SPENT TOO MUCH TIME WITH YOU GUYS, AND I WOULDN'T EAT YOU WHEN THE TIME CAME . . .

. . . I GUESS THEY WERE RIGHT.

THORN!

I . . . FEEL . . . SICK . .

GRAN'MA!

HONEY, WHAT'S WRONG?

I'LL BE ALL RIGHT.

HANG ON, THORN. WE'RE ALMOST THERE.

WHERE?

THE ONE PLACE IN ALL THE VALLEY THAT HASN'T SUCCUMBED TO THE GHOST CIRCLES.

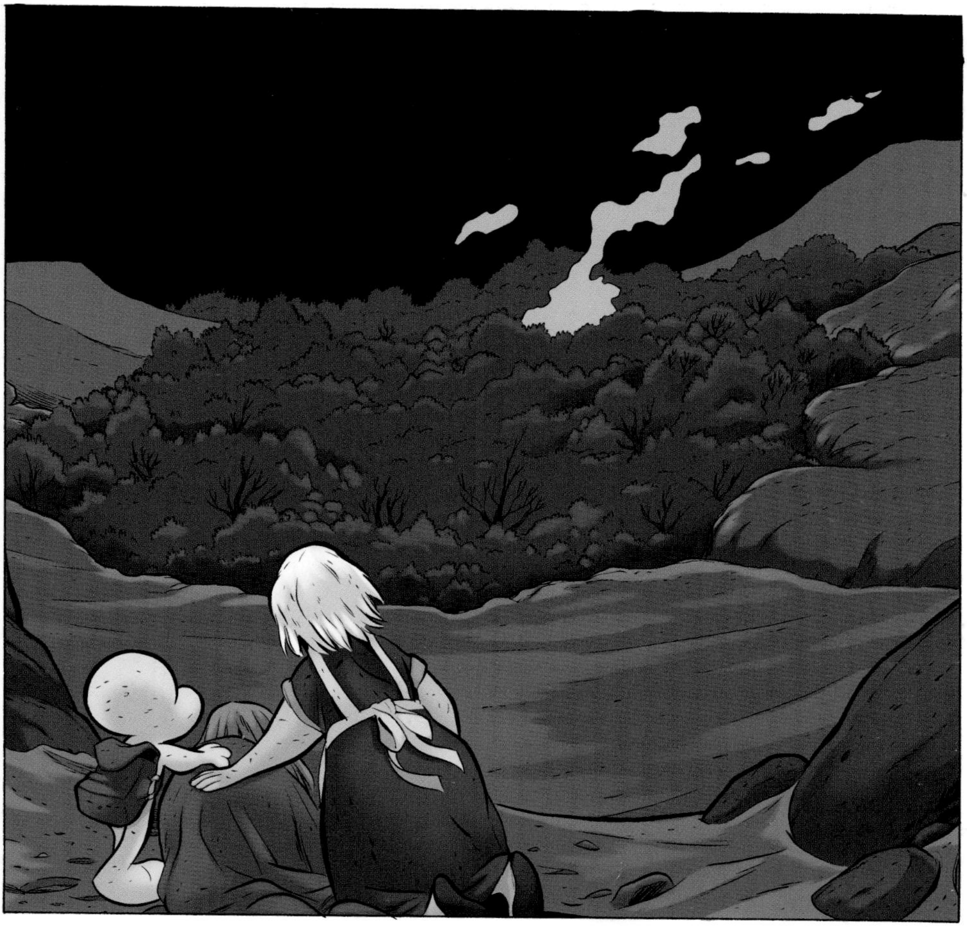

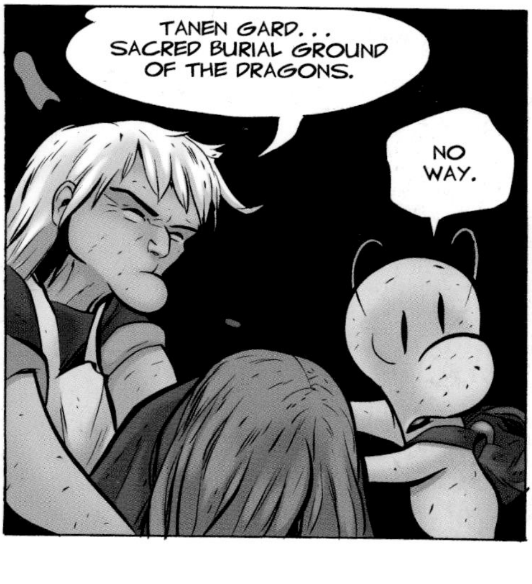
TANEN GARD. . . SACRED BURIAL GROUND OF THE DRAGONS.
NO WAY.

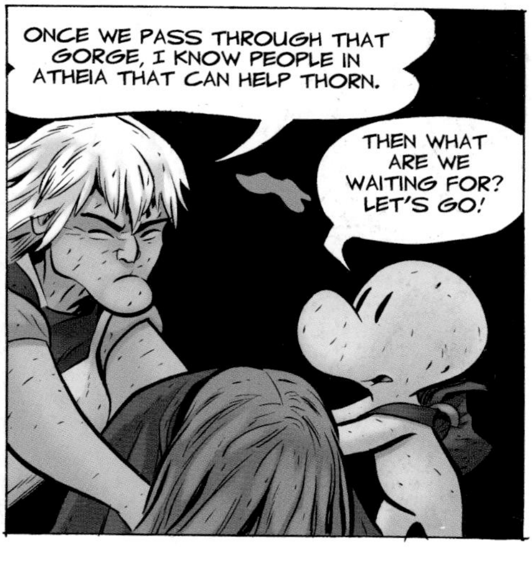
ONCE WE PASS THROUGH THAT GORGE, I KNOW PEOPLE IN ATHEIA THAT CAN HELP THORN.
THEN WHAT ARE WE WAITING FOR? LET'S GO!

BUT, GRAN'MA, I THINK THIS IS **SERIOUS** --

OF COURSE THIS IS **SERIOUS!** SHE HAS A PIECE OF THE **LOCUST** INSIDE HER!

I **KNOW** SHE HAS A PIECE OF THE LOCUST INSIDE HER -- THERE'S A PIECE INSIDE ME, **TOO**, REMEMBER?

THORN IS A **VENI-YAN-CARI**, BONE. SHE'S FAR MORE SENSITIVE TO EVIL THAN YOU OR I.

THAT'S WHY I'M **WORRIED**... WHEN WE WERE INSIDE THE GHOST CIRCLE, IT FELT LIKE SHE WAS TRYING TO **TAKE** THE PIECE THAT WAS INSIDE ME, AND PUT IT INSIDE HERSELF!

WHAT?! DID SHE **TOUCH IT?** WHY DIDN'T YOU **SAY** SOMETHING?

I AM SAYING SOMETHING --

... THE HOODED ONE ...

... IS COMING ...

WHAT WAS THAT, THORN?

THE HOODED ONE ...

SHE KNOWS WHERE WE ARE... SHE'S COMING ...

HANG ON, DEAR. THE CITY OF ATHEIA ISN'T FAR NOW.

COME ON, BONE. ONCE WE CROSS THIS GORGE, WE'LL BE PAST THE **GHOST CIRCLES** AND SHE'LL BE IN LESS DANGER.

I CAN'T BELIEVE WE'RE TRESPASSING ON THE SACRED DRAGON **BURIAL GROUNDS** LIKE THIS.

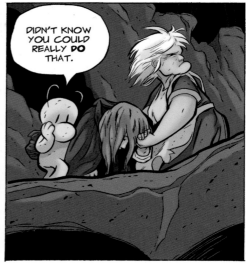

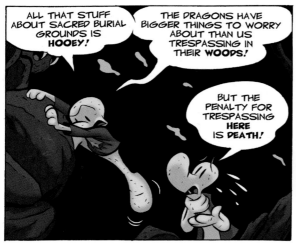

ALL THAT STUFF ABOUT SACRED BURIAL GROUNDS IS **HOOEY!**

THE DRAGONS HAVE BIGGER THINGS TO WORRY ABOUT THAN US TRESPASSING IN THEIR **WOODS!**

BUT THE PENALTY FOR TRESPASSING **HERE** IS **DEATH!**

DON'T THINK ABOUT THAT! THINK ABOUT ALL THE NICE **STUFF** YOU'RE GONNA EAT ONCE WE GET TO ATHEIA. **ROAST BEEF, MASHED POTATOES . . .**

AND A SOFT BED . . . WITH CLEAN **SHEETS. . .**

OKAY. BUT WHEN THE DANGER'S OVER, CAN WE GO HOME TO **BONEVILLE?**

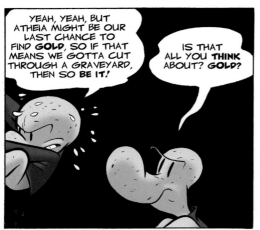

YEAH, YEAH, BUT ATHEIA MIGHT BE OUR LAST CHANCE TO FIND **GOLD**, SO IF THAT MEANS WE GOTTA CUT THROUGH A GRAVEYARD, THEN SO **BE IT!**

IS THAT ALL YOU **THINK** ABOUT? **GOLD?**

YES, **THAT'S ALL I THINK ABOUT!** AND JUST **LET** ME DO TH' THINKING, AN' WE'LL **BOTH** BE BETTER OFF.

GIMME A HAND, WILL YA? I CAN'T REACH.

REMEMBER! YOU'LL NEVER GET **ANYWHERE** WITHOUT **ME!**

YES, PHONEY.

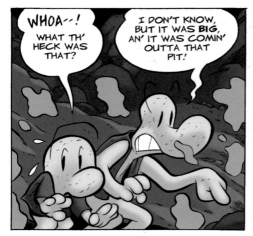

WHOA--! WHAT TH' HECK WAS THAT?

I DON'T KNOW, BUT IT WAS **BIG**, AN' IT WAS COMIN' OUTTA THAT PIT!

LOOK AT **BARTLEBY!**

IT'S THE DRAGONS! CAN'T YOU SMELL THE **BRIMSTONE?** IT'S EVERYWHERE!

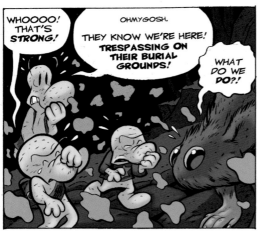

WHOOOO! THAT'S **STRONG!**

OHMYGOSH. THEY KNOW WE'RE HERE! **TRESPASSING ON THEIR BURIAL GROUNDS!**

WHAT DO WE **DO?!**

I DON'T **KNOW!**

I THINK IT MIGHT BE A GOOD IDEA IF WE KEEP OUR VOICES DOWN.

THERE'S THE **BRIDGE!**

RUN FOR IT!

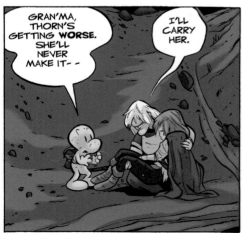

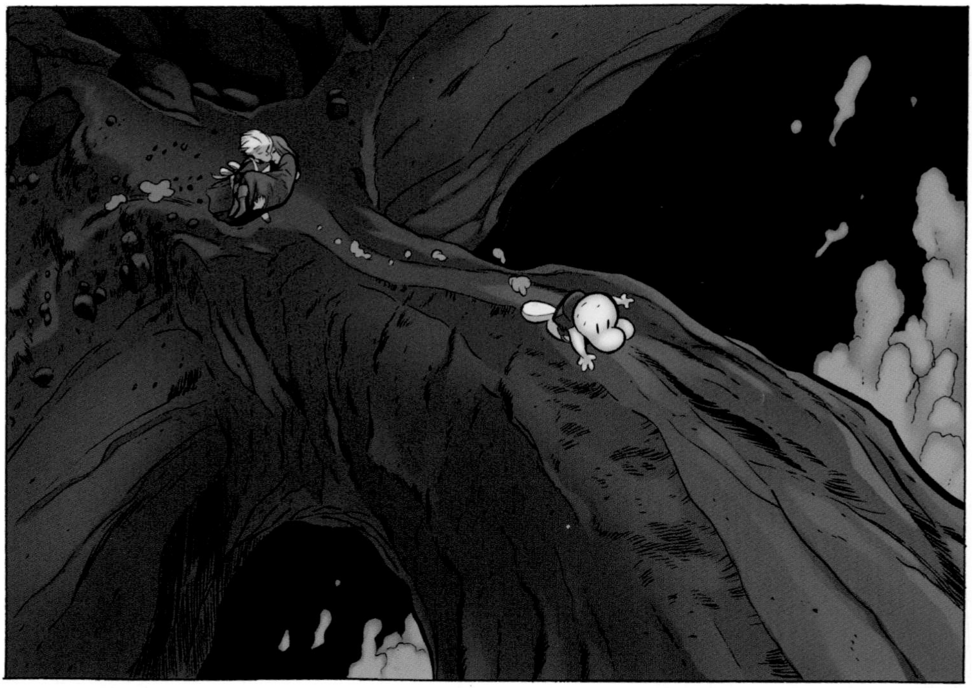

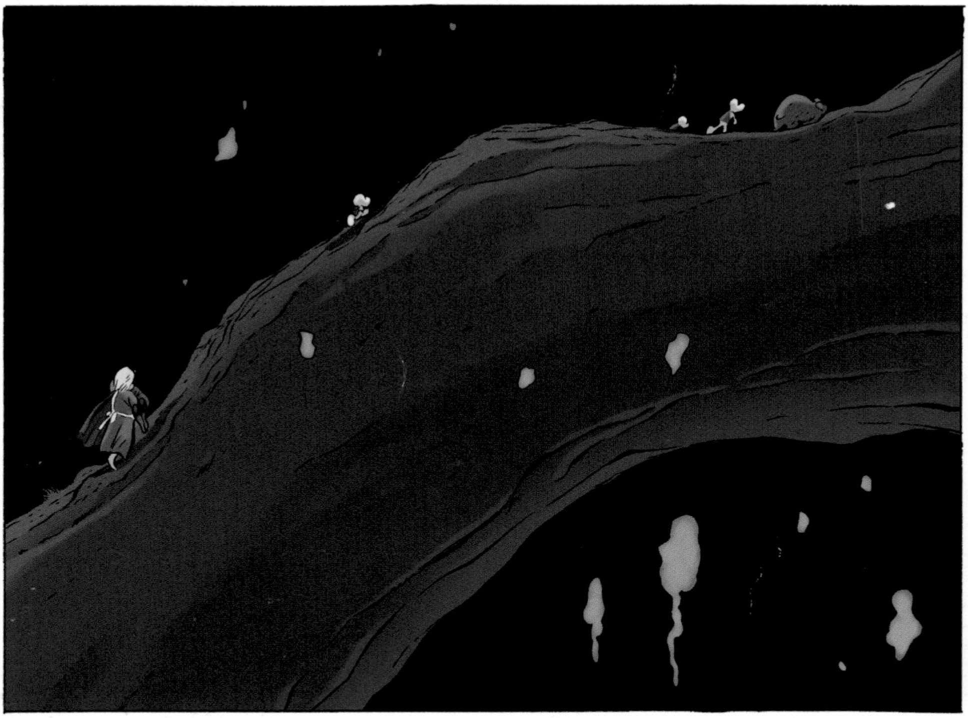

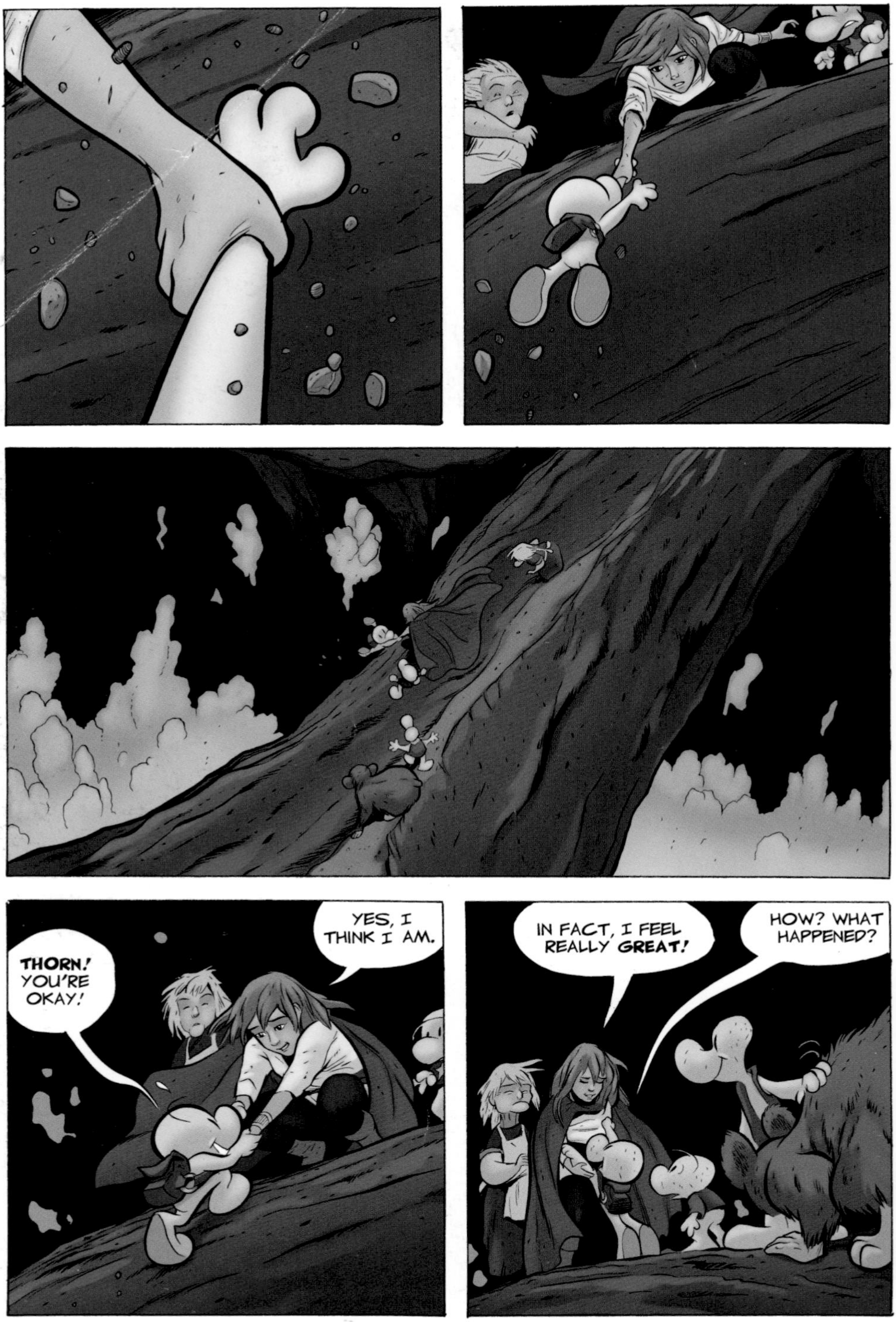
THORN! YOU'RE OKAY!
YES, I THINK I AM.
IN FACT, I FEEL REALLY GREAT!
HOW? WHAT HAPPENED?

IT'S THIS PLACE. SOMEHOW IT'S **HEALING** YOU.

YES, IT MAY BE.

COME! WE'RE ALMOST TO THE OTHER SIDE!

WE **MADE** IT!

IS THAT IT? ARE WE **OUT?**

THAT'S IT! WE MADE IT THROUGH **TANEN GARD!**

I CAN'T BELIEVE IT! NO ONE HAS EVER COME THROUGH THERE ALIVE.

MAN! THAT WASN'T **SO TOUGH!** EXCEPT FOR THE PART WHERE FONE BONE ALMOST BIT IT.

THERE'S MORE GOOD NEWS...

WE'RE PAST THE **GHOST CIRCLES!**

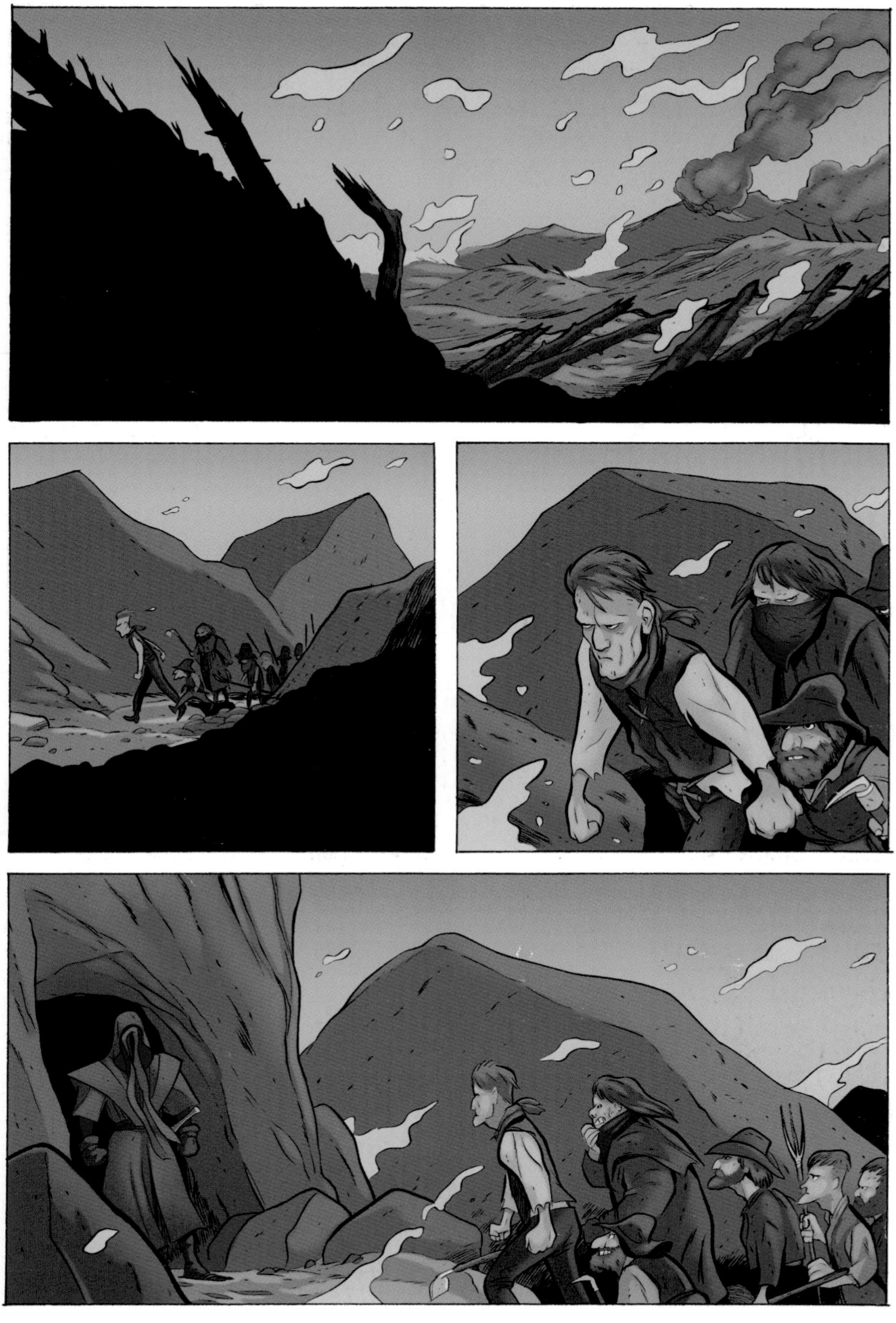

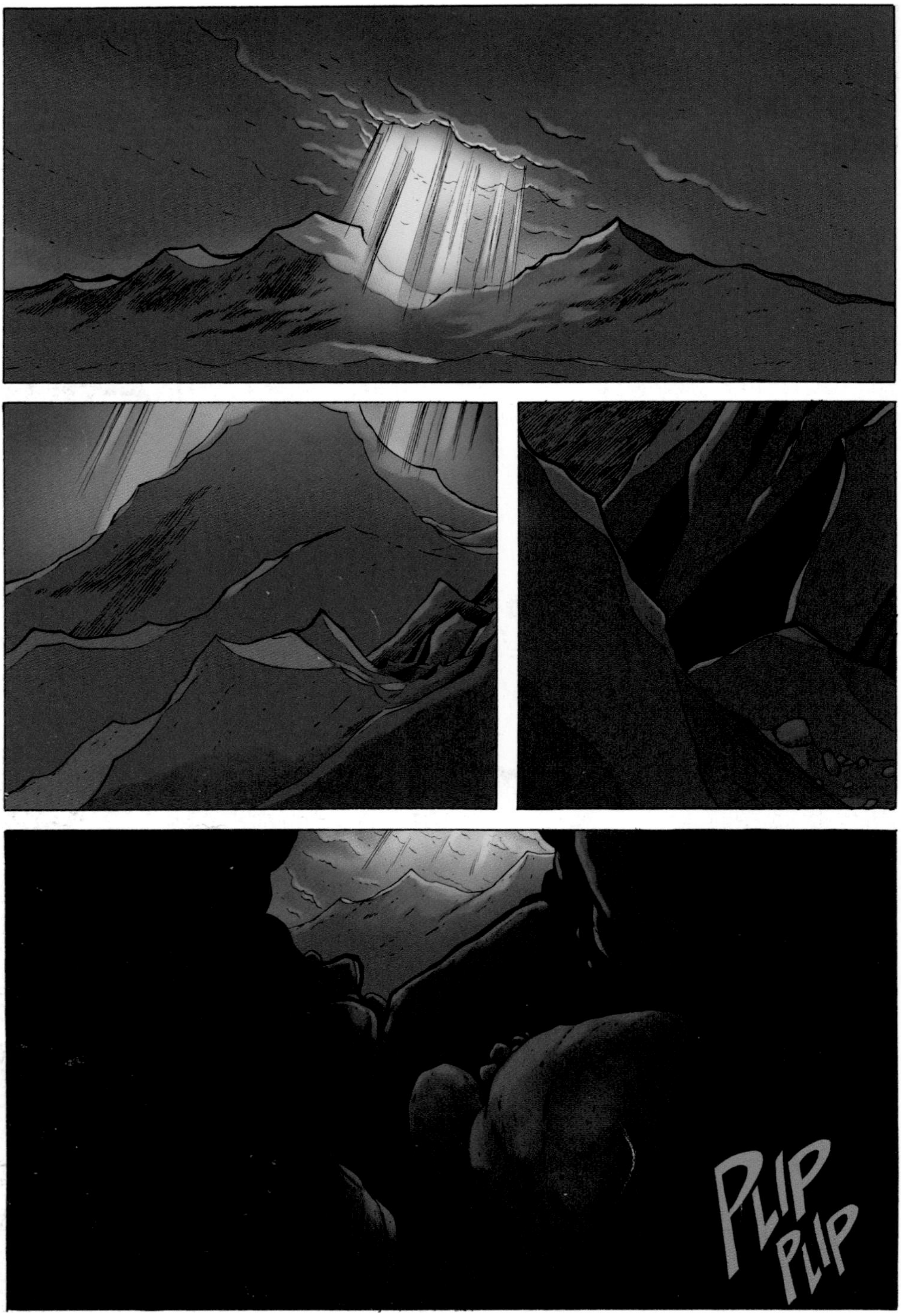
PLIP
PLIP

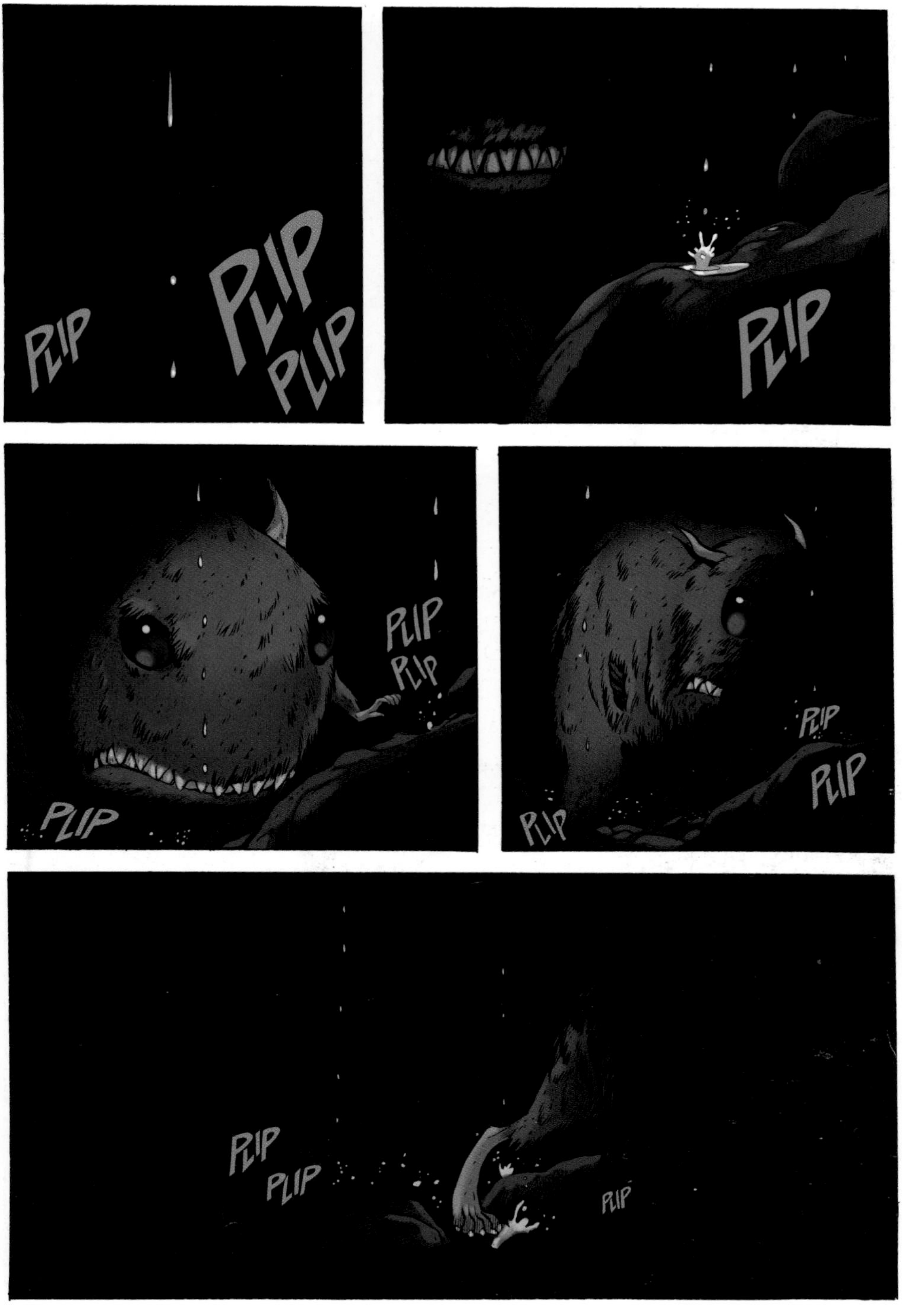
PLIP
PLIP
PLIP
PLIP
PLIP
PLIP
PLIP
PLIP
PLIP
PLIP
PLIP
PLIP
PLIP

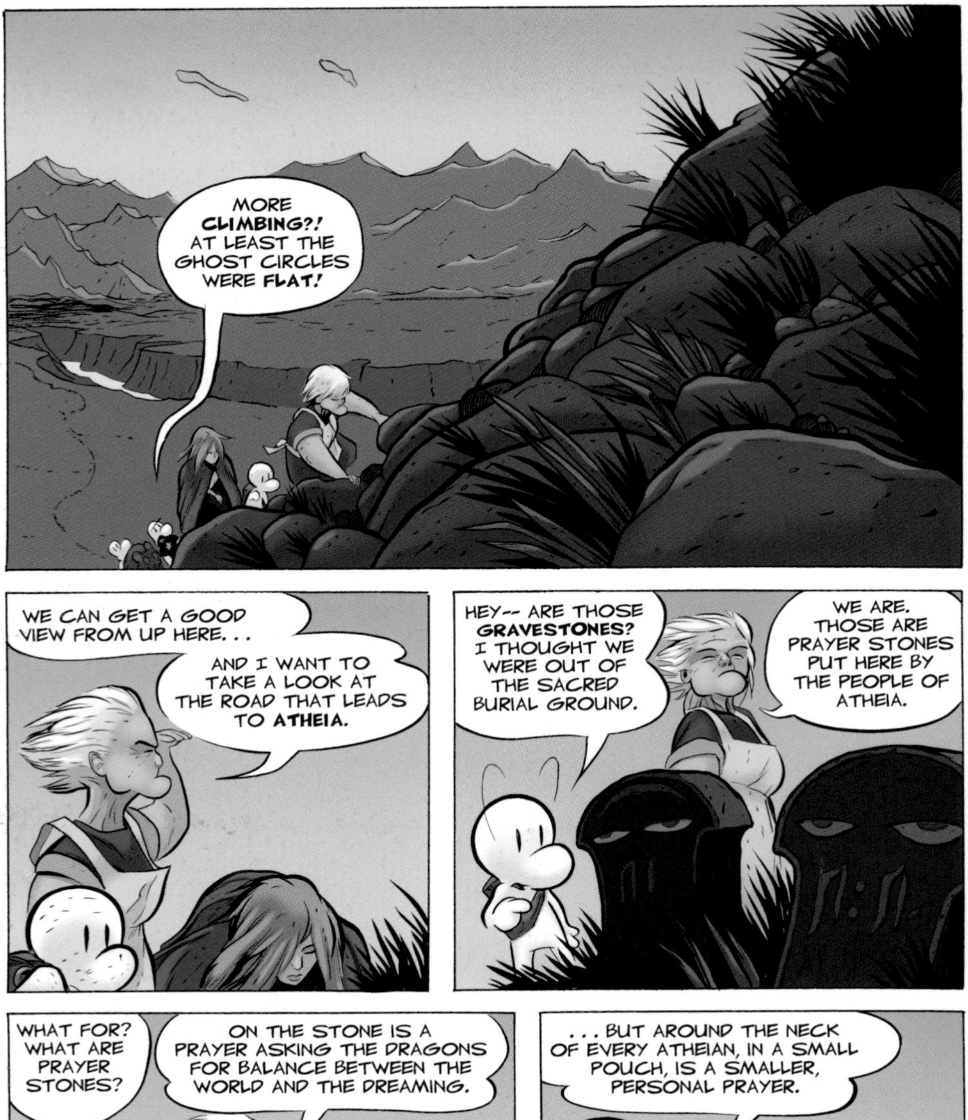
MORE **CLIMBING?!** AT LEAST THE GHOST CIRCLES WERE **FLAT!**
WE CAN GET A GOOD VIEW FROM UP HERE. . .
AND I WANT TO TAKE A LOOK AT THE ROAD THAT LEADS TO **ATHEIA**.
HEY-- ARE THOSE **GRAVESTONES?** I THOUGHT WE WERE OUT OF THE SACRED BURIAL GROUND.
WE ARE. THOSE ARE PRAYER STONES PUT HERE BY THE PEOPLE OF ATHEIA.
WHAT FOR? WHAT ARE PRAYER STONES?
ON THE STONE IS A PRAYER ASKING THE DRAGONS FOR BALANCE BETWEEN THE WORLD AND THE DREAMING.
THESE ARE THE BIG ONES. . .
. . . BUT AROUND THE NECK OF EVERY ATHEIAN, IN A SMALL POUCH, IS A SMALLER, PERSONAL PRAYER.

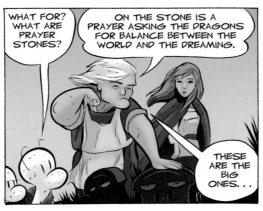

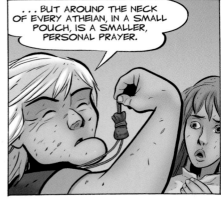

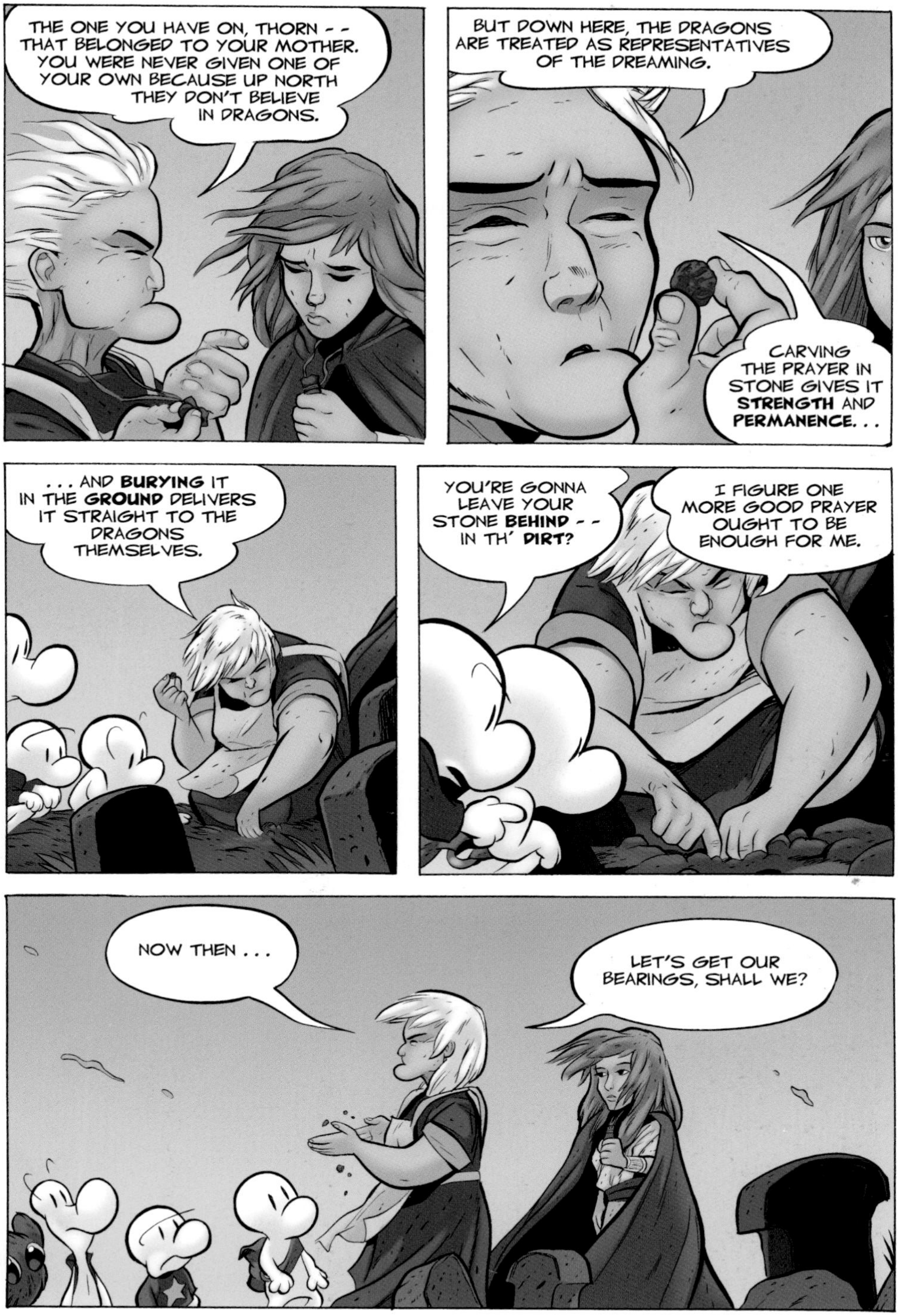
THE ONE YOU HAVE ON, THORN -- THAT BELONGED TO YOUR MOTHER. YOU WERE NEVER GIVEN ONE OF YOUR OWN BECAUSE UP NORTH THEY DON'T BELIEVE IN DRAGONS.
BUT DOWN HERE, THE DRAGONS ARE TREATED AS REPRESENTATIVES OF THE DREAMING.
CARVING THE PRAYER IN STONE GIVES IT **STRENGTH** AND **PERMANENCE**...
...AND **BURYING** IT IN THE **GROUND** DELIVERS IT STRAIGHT TO THE DRAGONS THEMSELVES.
YOU'RE GONNA LEAVE YOUR STONE **BEHIND** -- IN TH' **DIRT**?
I FIGURE ONE MORE GOOD PRAYER OUGHT TO BE ENOUGH FOR ME.
NOW THEN...
LET'S GET OUR BEARINGS, SHALL WE?

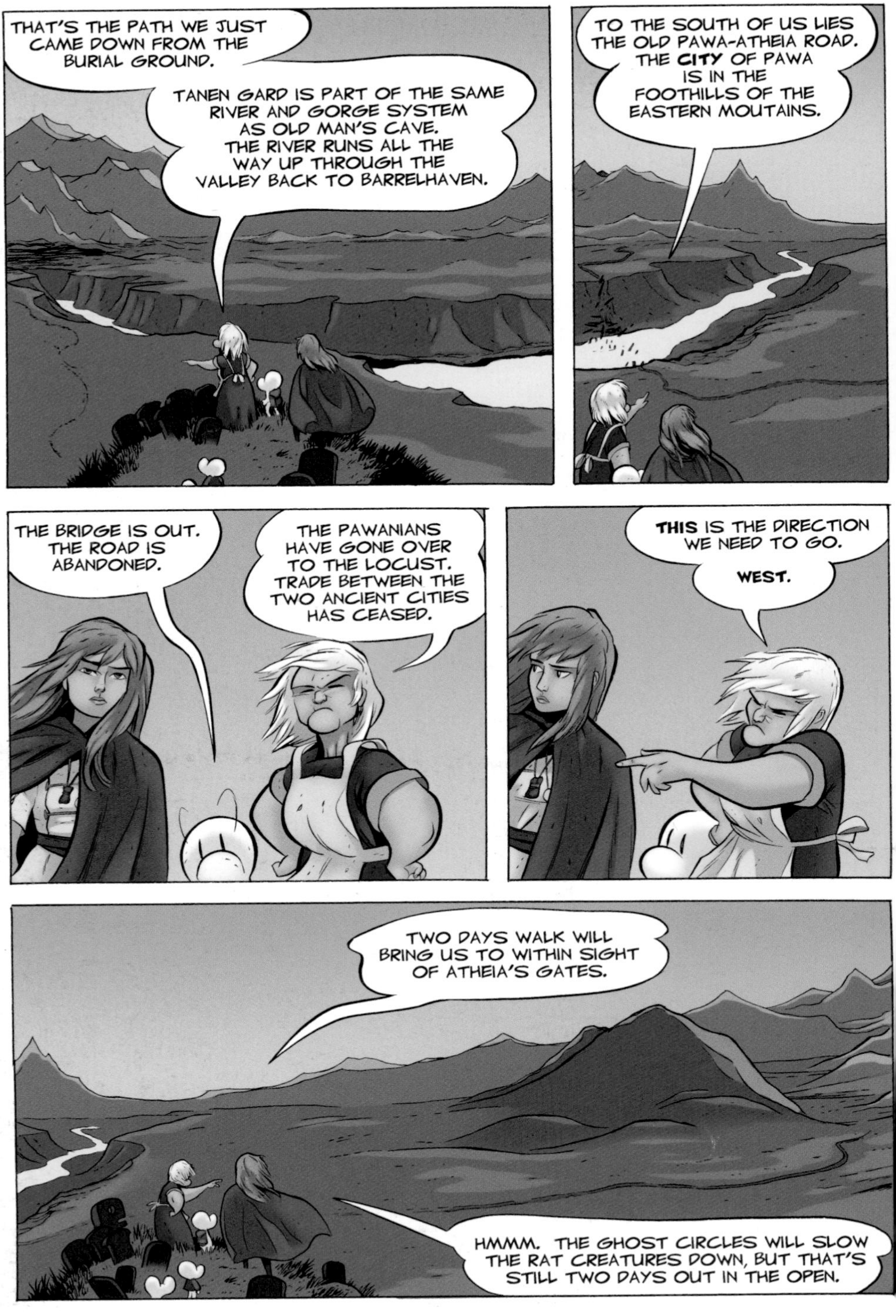
THAT'S THE PATH WE JUST CAME DOWN FROM THE BURIAL GROUND.
TANEN GARD IS PART OF THE SAME RIVER AND GORGE SYSTEM AS OLD MAN'S CAVE. THE RIVER RUNS ALL THE WAY UP THROUGH THE VALLEY BACK TO BARRELHAVEN.
TO THE SOUTH OF US LIES THE OLD PAWA-ATHEIA ROAD. THE **CITY** OF PAWA IS IN THE FOOTHILLS OF THE EASTERN MOUTAINS.
THE BRIDGE IS OUT. THE ROAD IS ABANDONED.
THE PAWANIANS HAVE GONE OVER TO THE LOCUST. TRADE BETWEEN THE TWO ANCIENT CITIES HAS CEASED.
THIS IS THE DIRECTION WE NEED TO GO.
WEST.
TWO DAYS WALK WILL BRING US TO WITHIN SIGHT OF ATHEIA'S GATES.
HMMM. THE GHOST CIRCLES WILL SLOW THE RAT CREATURES DOWN, BUT THAT'S STILL TWO DAYS OUT IN THE OPEN.

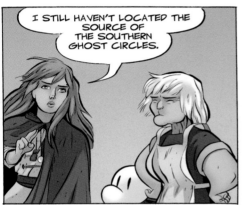

...TO BE CONTINUED.

About JEFF SMITH

JEFF SMITH was born and raised in the American Midwest and learned about cartooning from comic strips, comic books, and watching animated shorts on TV. After four years of drawing comic strips for The Ohio State University's student newspaper and co-founding Character Builders animation studio in 1986, Smith launched the comic book *BONE* in 1991. Between *BONE* and other comics projects, Smith spends much of his time on the international guest circuit promoting comics and the art of graphic novels.

More about *BONE*

An instant classic when it first appeared in the U.S. as an underground comic book in 1991, *BONE* has since garnered 38 international awards and sold a million copies in 15 languages. Now, Scholastic's GRAPHIX imprint is publishing full-color graphic novel editions of the nine-book *BONE* series. Look for the continuing adventures of the Bone cousins in *Treasure Hunters*.